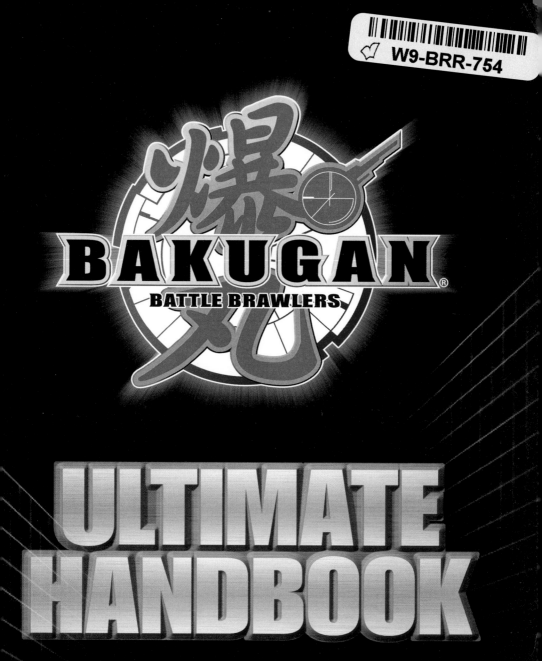

BAKUGAN
BATTLE BRAWLERS

ULTIMATE HANDBOOK

by Tracey West

SCHOLASTIC INC.
New York   Toronto   London   Auckland
Sydney   Mexico City   New Delhi   Hong Kong

ATTENTION, BAKUGAN MASTERS!

We need your help to improve our records in the
Official Bakugan Ultimate Handbook Hunt!

There are more Bakugan to be found and identified
beyond the ones listed in the book!

If you have a Bakugan that you think is missing from
this handbook, go to www.bakugan.com and tell us what
you have found. You can learn a lot more about the ways
to play Bakugan, learn cool moves, and see all the best
Bakugan action. If you're lucky, you might see your
Bakugan in the next handbook!

And don't forget to unleash your Bakugan online in
Bakugan Dimensions!

ISBN 978-0-545-25181-5

12 11 10 9 8 7 6 5 4 3 2   10 11 12 13 14 15/0

Printed in the U.S.A.
First printing, September 2010

THE ULTIMATE WORD ON BAKUGAN

Whether you are new to Bakugan or if you've been playing since the first cards fell from the sky, this book has all the info you need to become a top-ranked Bakugan brawler.

In the first section, you'll find all of the Bakugan from Series 1, including Starters and Boosters and Special Attack Bakugan. Section Two covers the New Vestroia Bakugan, including Bakugan Traps. And for the first time ever, you'll get the scoop on the new Series 3 Bakugan from Gundalian Invaders.

In the last section you'll read about some surprising new additions to the world of Bakugan, including Battle Gear that can give you an edge over your opponents. And we saved the biggest surprise for last: Dragonoid Colossus, the largest, most powerful form of Drago ever created.

There's so much info you'll need more heads than a Hydranoid to remember it all! But don't sweat it — there's more than one way to use this book. If you're like Marucho, you can read it all the way through, taking notes while developing your newest strategy. If you're more like Dan, you can stash it in your pocket and bring it out during battle when things get tough.

Whatever you do, don't forget to check out all of the new and exciting Bakugan inside. There's a whole new world waiting for you!

PLAY THE GAME

To play, you need at least two players and three Bakugan, three Gate cards, and three Ability cards each. You must have one of each type of Gate card (silver, copper, and gold) and one of each type of Ability card (red, blue, and green). The first player to collect three Gate cards in his or her used pile is the winner!

STEP 1: BEGIN

For a game with two players, sit facing one another across the battlefield. Each player should create a space on the right for unused Gate cards, Ability cards, and Bakugan (the "unused pile") and a space on the left for used Gate cards, Ability cards, and Bakugan (the "used pile"). Each player selects one Gate card and places it facedown in the middle of the battlefield, on the side closest to his or her opponent.

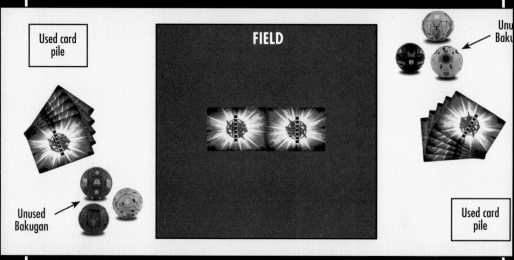

Used card pile

FIELD

Unu
Baku

Unused Bakugan

Used card pile

STEP 2: SHOOT

The youngest player goes first—that's Player 1. Player 1 shoots a Bakugan. Make sure your Bakugan is two card lengths away from the facedown card. Then roll your Bakugan onto the field. Player 1 also has the option of playing an Ability card before shooting. Each Ability card indicates when it can be played: before, during, or after a battle.

STEP 3: BRAWL!

Player 2 shoots a Bakugan. Player 1 and Player 2 take turns until they each have a Bakugan standing on the same Gate card. Then it's time to brawl! Flip over the Gate card. Look at the number showing on each Bakugan. That number tells you how many Gs each Bakugan has.

What Happens If . . .

. . . one player has two Bakugan stand on the same card? If there are two Gate cards on the field, the player can decide which Bakugan to move to the other Gate card. If there is only one Gate card on the field, the player automatically captures the card.

STEP 4: CARD EFFECTS

If the Gate card has any text on it, do whatever it says. Then players may play any of their Ability cards in their unused pile that are playable during battle, applying whatever effects they might have. After playing an Ability card, it is moved to the player's used pile. When both players have played all the Ability cards they want, move on to Step 5.

STEP 5: GATE CARD G-POWER BOOST

Each Bakugan adds the Gate Card G-Power Boost that matches the Bakugan's attribute to their Bakugan's current G-Power. These attribute bonuses are found in the 6 circles on the left hand side of the Gate card.

STEP 6: WINNING

The Bakugan with the highest G-power after Gate attribute bonuses wins the battle. The winner moves the Gate card and their own Bakugn to their used pile. The other player moves their Bakugan to their own used pile. BAKUGAN NEVER GO TO YOUR OPPONENT'S USED PILE! (And no, your friend doesn't get to keep your defeated Bakugan after the game either!)

What Happens If . . .

. . . there is a tie? The player who rolled onto the card first automatically wins!

STEP 7: TAKE TURNS

End of round one! To keep playing, continue taking turns, aiming for the remaining Gate card on the field. If Player 1 was the last to roll, it's now Player 2's turn. Take turns rolling until a new battle starts, then follow the instructions from Steps 3-6.

STEP 8: NEW GATE CARDS

Once you've battled a second time, leaving no Gate cards remaining on the field, each player places another Gate card from their unused pile facedown in the middle of the field on the side closest to his or her opponent — exactly the same way as in Step 1. Then the battle continues!

What Happens If . . .

. . . one player runs out of Bakugan in their unused pile to roll? When this happens, the player closes all of their Bakugan in their used pile and moves them all to their unused pile.

STEP 9: THE WINNER!

Keep playing until one player has three Gate cards in his or her used pile. That player is the winner. Congratulations!

BAKUGAN TRAP AND BAKUGAN BATTLE GEAR

The new season of Bakugan is packed with amazing game-changers, including Bakugan Battle Gear. Both your Trap and Battle Gear starts in the unused pile. You can have up to two Battle Gear and/or Traps in a game.

A Bakugan Trap may be played in any battle as long as you have a Bakugan in the battle and the trap is the same attribute as the Bakugan in play.

When the trap is dropped onto the Gate card, it will pop open and reveal one or more attribute icons. You can then switch the attribute of the Bakugan to any of the new attributes revealed!

To use your gear, place it on the back of your Bakugan to open it. Bakugan Battle Gear may also be opened on a Gate card, like a Trap. Once the gear is open, add the G-Power revealed on the inside of your Bakugan Battle Gear to your battling Bakugan. If your Bakugan's attribute matches either of the attributes on your reference card, then you get that ability as well!

If your Gear matches the color of the Gate card (bronze, silver, or copper), you can choose any one ability on the reference card to use in this battle.

After the battle, your Gear and/or Trap is moved to the used pile. If you must move Bakugan from the used pile to the unused pile in order to have a Bakugan to roll, move any Gear and/or Trap to the unused pile as well.

WHERE IT ALL BEGAN

In Dan Kuso's world, Bakugan balls dropped from the sky one day, and kids everywhere started playing the game. One day they were regular kids, and the next, they were Battle Brawlers.

In our world, Bakugan became popular just as quickly. In these first battles, kids used Series 1 Bakugan. In this section you'll get a description of all of the Series 1 Starters and Boosters as well as the very first Special Attack Bakugan.

Starters and Boosters are the building blocks for any masterful team of Bakugan. Special Attack Bakugan give any brawler an extra boost of power.

APOLLONIR

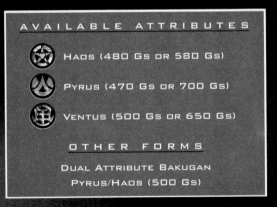

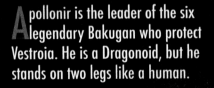pollonir is the leader of the six legendary Bakugan who protect Vestroia. He is a Dragonoid, but he stands on two legs like a human.

SEEN WITH: DAN KUSO.
WHEN DAN'S DRAGO WAS
TAKEN BY SPECTRA,
APOLLONIR OFFERED TO
BECOME DAN'S GUARDIAN
BAKUGAN UNTIL THEY
COULD GET DRAGO BACK.

AVAILABLE ATTRIBUTES

- HAOS (480 GS OR 580 GS)
- PYRUS (470 GS OR 700 GS)
- VENTUS (500 GS OR 650 GS)

OTHER FORMS

DUAL ATTRIBUTE BAKUGAN
PYRUS/HAOS (500 GS)

BEE STRIKER

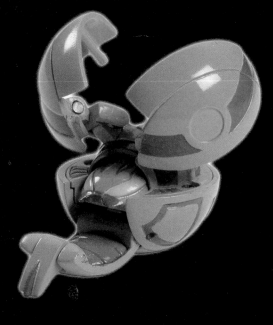

Get out your bug spray! If Bee Striker gets you with its poisonous stinger, the battle's over. Bee Striker can also flap its wings with amazing speed, creating a tornado to blow its opponents off the field.

SEEN WITH: MANY BRAWLERS INCLUDING ALICE, WHO USED A VENTUS BEE STRIKER IN A BATTLE AGAINST KLAUS.

AVAILABLE ATTRIBUTES

- Aquos (540 Gs or 600 Gs)
- Haos (350 Gs, 430 Gs, or 500 Gs)
- Pyrus (320 Gs or 640 Gs)
- Ventus (380 Gs or 480 Gs)

OTHER FORMS

Bakuflip Ventus (430 Gs)

BLADE TIGRERRA

When Blade Tigrerra evolves, she can stand on her hind legs. This allows her to better lock in her opponent's position on the battlefield. When Blade Tigrerra bounces, she slashes at foes with her sharp claws, long fangs, and the curved blades that protrude from her body.

SEEN WITH: DAN'S FRIEND RUNO. HER GUARDIAN BAKUGAN, HAOS TIGRERRA, EVOLVED INTO BLADE TIGRERRA IN A BATTLE IN THE DOOM DIMENSION.

EVOLUTION
CHAIN

TIGRERRA

≫

BLADE TIGRERRA

AVAILABLE ATTRIBUTES

HAOS (440 GS, 510 GS, OR 590 GS)

SUBTERRA (450 GS OR 550 GS)

VENTUS (350 GS OR 450 GS)

OTHER FORMS

CLEAR (580 GS), BAKUPEARL HAOS (500 GS)

CENTIPOID

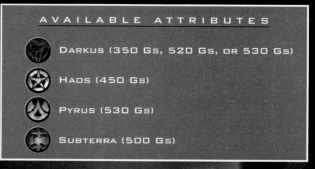

Don't think you can squash this creepy crawly creature with your shoe—Centipoid is one tough Bakugan. Its hard outer skeleton is like armor. It can slash at opponents with its two razorlike pincers and sharp twin tails. Centipoid can sense an enemy that's miles away using its antennae. Then it digs underground and bursts out of the earth to catch its foe by surprise.

SEEN WITH: POP STAR BRAWLER JEWLS, WHO USES A SUBTERRA CENTIPOID.

AVAILABLE ATTRIBUTES

- DARKUS (350 Gs, 520 Gs, OR 530 Gs)
- HAOS (450 Gs)
- PYRUS (530 Gs)
- SUBTERRA (500 Gs)

CLAYF

This massive warrior is the strongest of the legendary soldiers. Clayf uses a long-staffed lochbar axe to pummel opponents and shield itself from attacks. But that's not all Clayf can do. If an opponent gets an ability on the field, Clayf can absorb that ability!

SEEN WITH: THE SIX LEGENDARY SOLDIERS OF VESTROIA.

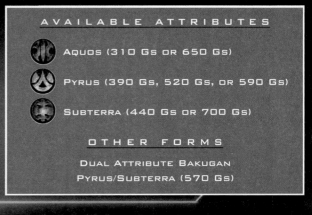

AVAILABLE ATTRIBUTES

AQUOS (310 Gs OR 650 Gs)

PYRUS (390 Gs, 520 Gs, OR 590 Gs)

SUBTERRA (440 Gs OR 700 Gs)

OTHER FORMS

DUAL ATTRIBUTE BAKUGAN
PYRUS/SUBTERRA (570 Gs)

CYCLOID

390g

AVAILABLE ATTRIBUTES

Darkus (390 Gs or 570 Gs)

Subterra (470 Gs or 510 Gs)

Ventus (400 Gs or 580 Gs)

OTHER FORMS

Clear (510 Gs)

Just like the legendary monster Cyclops, Cycloid has one lone eye in the middle of his forehead. He's also a gigantic brute with super strength. Cycloid attacks with the horn on his head and his large club. This big brute is always up for a battle!

SEEN WITH: JULIE'S FRIEND AND TOP-RANKED BRAWLER, BILLY. HIS GUARDIAN BAKUGAN IS A SUBTERRA CYCLOID.

DRAGONOID

Even though Dragonoid gets more and more powerful with each evolved form, his original form is one to be reckoned with. He can raise so much fiery energy during battle that everything around him melts. His unusually high intelligence allows him to use strategy on the field. Dragonoid's main weakness is that he's not extremely agile, but what he loses in mobility he makes up for with his powerful strikes.

SEEN WITH: DAN KUSO. WHEN DAN FIRST MET HIS PYRUS GUARDIAN BAKUGAN, DRAGO, HE WAS IN HIS DRAGONOID FORM.

AVAILABLE ATTRIBUTES

DARKUS (400 Gs)

PYRUS (300 Gs, 350 Gs, 450 Gs, OR 600 Gs)

SUBTERRA (450 Gs OR 470 Gs)

VENTUS (350 Gs OR 560 Gs)

OTHER FORMS

BakuBronze Pyrus (600 Gs), BakuFlip Pyrus (400 Gs)
BakuLyte Darkus (540 Gs), BakuLyte Pyrus (480 Gs)
BakuLyte Subterra (480 Gs), Deka Aquos (450 Gs)
Deka Darkus (450 Gs), Deka Haos (450 Gs), Deka Pyrus (450 Gs)
Deka Ventus (450 Gs), Clear (570 Gs), Heavy Metal Darkus (350 Gs)
Heavy Metal Haos (650 Gs), Heavy Metal Pyrus (670 Gs)

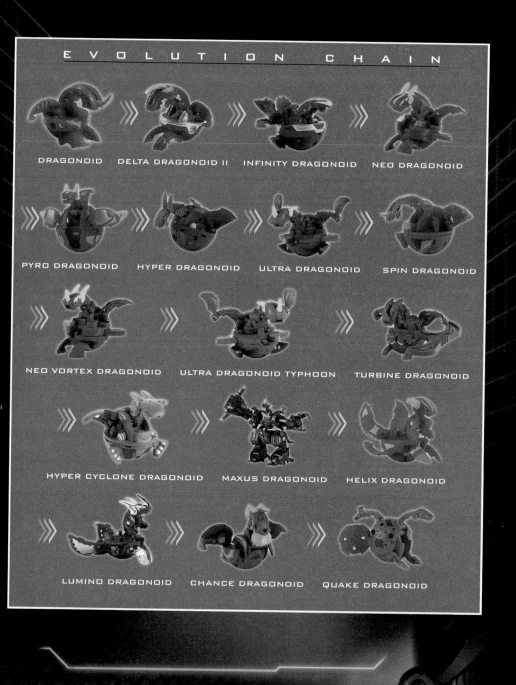

DUAL HYDRANOID

HYDRANOID

DUAL HYDRANOID

ALPHA HYDRANOID

This Bakugan is extremely strong, and it steals energy from Bakugan sent to the Doom Dimension to become stronger. Only a cruel and heartless creature could do that! In battle, Hydranoid is hard to defeat, thanks to its tough outer skin and double heads. It lashes out at opponents with its long tail. Hydranoid may not be able to move fast, but it makes up for its lack of speed with the sheer force of its attacks.

SEEN WITH:
MASQUERADE.

AVAILABLE ATTRIBUTES

- Aquos (540 Gs or 450 Gs)
- Darkus (450 Gs or 600 Gs)
- Pyrus (380 Gs or 450Gs)

OTHER FORMS
BakuFlip Darkus (420 Gs, 580 Gs, or 650 Gs)
BakuFlip Subterra (550 Gs), BakuFlip Ventus (520 Gs)
BakuLyte Darkus (500 Gs or 640 Gs)
BakuLyte Pyrus (530 Gs), Heavy Metal Aquos (530 Gs)
Heavy Metal Darkus (520 Gs)
Heavy Metal Haos (250 Gs)
Heavy Metal Pyrus (350 Gs or 540 Gs)

EL CONDOR

AVAILABLE ATTRIBUTES

AQUOS (490 Gs)

DARKUS (340 Gs, 400 Gs, OR 560 Gs)

PYRUS (380 Gs)

SUBTERRA (470 Gs OR 650 Gs)

VENTUS (430 Gs, 520 Gs, OR 660 Gs)

OTHER FORMS

BAKUPEARL SUBTERRA (420 Gs)

BAKUPEARL VENTUS (390 Gs)

BAKUFLIP SUBTERRA (420 Gs)

BAKUFLIP VENTUS (390 Gs)

CLEAR (500 Gs)

This Bakugan looks like a mysterious ancient statue. It can soar over the battlefield like the bird of prey it's named after. When El Condor attacks, it hits opponents with a bright laser beam.

SEEN WITH: MANY BRAWLERS, INCLUDING KOMBA, WHO USES A VENTUS EL CONDOR IN BATTLE.

EXEDRA

What's scarier than one snarling head full of sharp teeth? H eight? Exedra resembles a mythical multiheaded beast ca Hydra. The Greek monster had nine heads, but Exedra makes u missing head with one eye and a giant set of jaws in its chest. Exedra's heads can blast its opponents with deadly fire. In add amazing looks, Exedra has an amazing ability: It can transfer other Bakugan on the field to increase its own strength!

SEEN WITH: THE SIX LEGENDARY SOLDIERS OF VES

AVAILABLE ATTRIBUTES

 DARKUS (450 GS OR 660 GS)

SUBTERRA (400 GS OR 640 GS)

VENTUS (490 GS OR 530 GS)

OTHER FORMS

DUAL ATTRIBUTE BAKUGAN
DARKUS/VENTUS (490 GS)

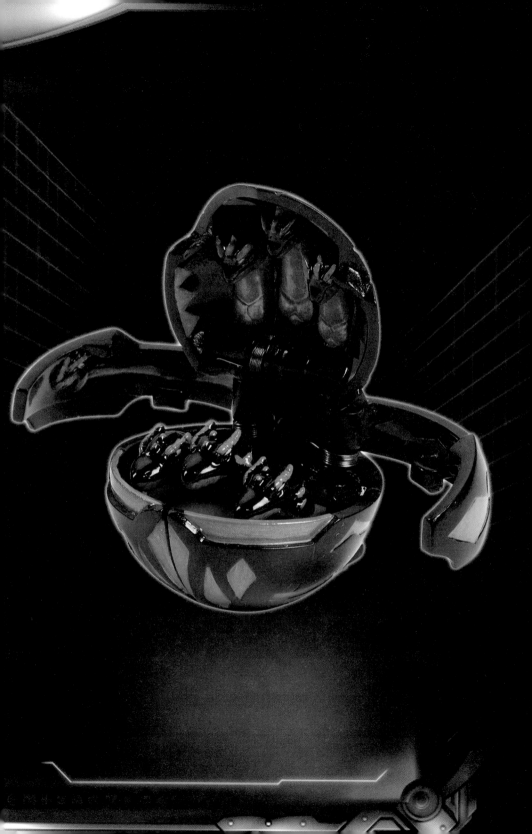

FALCONEER

It's not easy to defeat Falconeer. This fast-flying Bakugan can maneuver at high speed. It uses superior vision to target prey from a distance. And if you are lucky enough to bring Falconeer down—watch out! This amazing creature can resurrect itself and right any wrong it experienced during battle. Only the best brawlers can take down Falconeer twice.

SEEN WITH: SEVERAL BRAWLERS, INCLUDING DAN, WHO HAD A PYRUS FALCONEER, AND SHUN, WHO HAD A VENTUS FALCONEER.

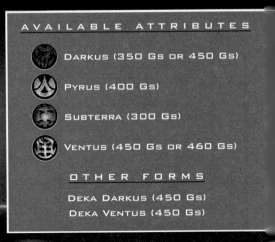

AVAILABLE ATTRIBUTES

- DARKUS (350 Gs OR 450 Gs)
- PYRUS (400 Gs)
- SUBTERRA (300 Gs)
- VENTUS (450 Gs OR 460 Gs)

OTHER FORMS

DEKA DARKUS (450 Gs)
DEKA VENTUS (450 Gs)

FEAR RIPPER

AVAILABLE ATTRIBUTES

- DARKUS (390 Gs, 450 Gs, 470 Gs)
- HAOS (310 Gs)
- PYRUS (300 Gs)
- SUBTERRA (540 Gs)

OTHER FORMS

BAKULYTE AQUOS (450 Gs)
WHITE (450 Gs)

Fear Ripper gets its name from its monstrous claws. Each one is three times bigger than its head! Fear Ripper can use them to slash its enemies on the battlefield.

SEEN WITH: MANY BRAWLERS, INCLUDING DUELING POP STAR JENNY, AND BULLYING BRAWLER SHUJI.

FORTRESS

This tall, muscled Bakugan has four arms and four faces. He uses his arms to wield the multiple weapons strapped to his back. Fortress' swords can shoot fire at his enemies. As the battle intensifies, Fortress can switch to a new face to match his emotion.

SEEN WITH: CHAN LEE. HAD A PYRUS FORTRESS AS HER GUARDIAN BAKUGAN.

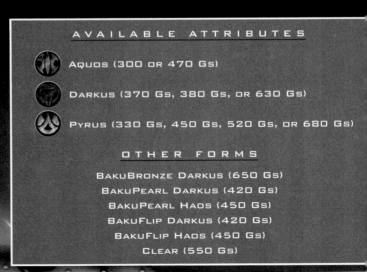

AVAILABLE ATTRIBUTES

AQUOS (300 OR 470 Gs)

DARKUS (370 Gs, 380 Gs, OR 630 Gs)

PYRUS (330 Gs, 450 Gs, 520 Gs, OR 680 Gs)

OTHER FORMS

BAKUBRONZE DARKUS (650 Gs)
BAKUPEARL DARKUS (420 Gs)
BAKUPEARL HAOS (450 Gs)
BAKUFLIP DARKUS (420 Gs)
BAKUFLIP HAOS (450 Gs)
CLEAR (550 Gs)

FROSCH

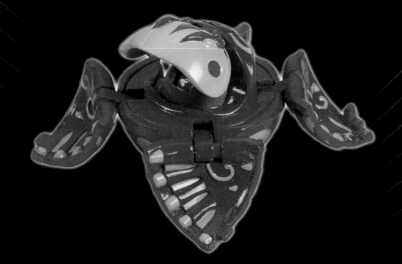

Frosch may look like a big, harmless frog, but his looks are deceiving. This legendary Bakugan is a force to be reckoned with on the battlefield. He's very wise, which means he's great at strategy. He can move quickly with his powerful legs, and lash out at opponents with his long tongue. He's got a lot of hidden power, too. Frosch can whip up a wild water tornado to take down his enemies!

SEEN WITH: THE SIX LEGENDARY SOLDIERS OF VESTROIA.

AVAILABLE ATTRIBUTES

- AQUOS (430 Gs OR 660 Gs)
- DARKUS (480 Gs OR 610 Gs)
- PYRUS (310 Gs OR 530 Gs)
- SUBTERRA (610 Gs)

OTHER FORMS

DUAL ATTRIBUTE BAKUGAN
PYRUS/AQUOS (610 Gs)

GARGONOID

Gargonoid resembles a gargoyle, one of those creepy stone statues mounted on buildings to scare off evil spirits. On the field, Gargonoid does a good job of scaring his opponents. His wings are tipped with sharp spikes. His long, curved horns are dangerous weapons and his clawed hands can shred just about anything in his path. Top that off with a scary gargoyle face and you've got one frightening foe!

SEEN WITH: MANY BRAWLERS, INCLUDING DAN AND CHAN LEE. THEY HAVE BOTH USED A PYRUS GARGONOID IN BATTLE.

AVAILABLE ATTRIBUTES

- AQUOS (390 Gs or 510 Gs)
- HAOS (270 Gs or 450 Gs)
- VENTUS (390 Gs, 400 Gs, or 570Gs)

OTHER FORMS

CLEAR (520 Gs)

GOREM

This giant is normally gentle, but it can get very angry in the heat of battle. When that happens, watch out! Gorem uses its massive fist to pound its opponents. Its strong shield can lower the G-Power of any Bakugan. Attackers have a hard time making a den n Gorem's hard body. That's because the cells in its body are very dense.

SEEN WITH: JULIE. A SUBTERRA GOREM IS HER GUARDIAN BAKUGAN.

AVAILABLE ATTRIBUTES

- AQUOS (480 Gs or 570 Gs)
- DARKUS (600 Gs)
- PYRUS (400 Gs)
- SUBTERRA (400 Gs, 450 Gs, 480 Gs, or 580 Gs)
- VENTUS (250 Gs, 430 Gs, 590 Gs)

OTHER FORMS

DEKA HAOS (450 Gs), DEKA SUBTERRA (450 Gs)

EVOLUTION CHAIN

GOREM

HAMMER GOREM

GRIFFON

Griffon looks like a mythical monster that's a combination of several animals. It's got the fierce head and claws of a lion, the powerful wings of an eagle, a tail that's a poisonous serpent, and the hard-kicking legs of a goat. Before Griffon lashes out with its claws or tail, it can emit a defeaning roar that will stun its opponent.

SEEN WITH: SEVERAL BRAWLERS, INCLUDING DAN. HE HAS USED MANY PYRUS GRIFFON IN BATTLE.

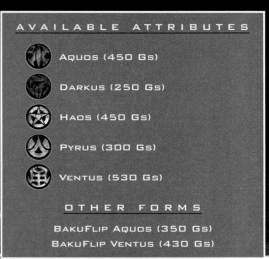

AVAILABLE ATTRIBUTES

Aquos (450 Gs)

Darkus (250 Gs)

Haos (450 Gs)

Pyrus (300 Gs)

Ventus (530 Gs)

OTHER FORMS

BakuFlip Aquos (350 Gs)
BakuFlip Ventus (430 Gs)

HAMMER GOREM

AVAILABLE ATTRIBUTES

- Darkus (600Gs)
- Haos (400 Gs or 530 Gs)
- Pyrus (420 Gs or 670 Gs)
- Subterra (480 Gs or 610 Gs)
- Ventus (590 Gs)

OTHER FORMS

BakuPearl Subterra (580 Gs)
BakuBronze Subterra (620 Gs)

When Gorem evolves, its shield transforms into a huge double-sided hammer. When Hammer Gorem uses this weapon, it causes ultimate destruction. Hammer Gorem also gains a protective coat of armor and bull-like horns on its head to intimidate its foes.

SEEN WITH: JULIE. HER GUARDIAN BAKUGAN GOREM EVOLVED INTO HAMMER GOREM.

FOR EVOLUTION CHAIN, FLIP TO PAGE 27.

HARPUS

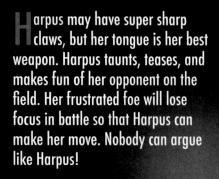

Harpus may have super sharp claws, but her tongue is her best weapon. Harpus taunts, teases, and makes fun of her opponent on the field. Her frustrated foe will lose focus in battle so that Harpus can make her move. Nobody can argue like Harpus!

SEEN WITH: TOP-RANKED BRAWLER KOMBA. HIS GUARDIAN BAKUGAN IS A VENTUS HARPUS.

AVAILABLE ATTRIBUTES

- AQUOS (400 Gs)
- DARKUS (400 Gs OR 650 Gs)
- HAOS (290 Gs OR 520 Gs)
- PYRUS (550 Gs)
- VENTUS (300 Gs OR 610 Gs)

OTHER FORMS

BAKUFLIP PYRUS (400 Gs)
BAKUPEARL PYRUS (400 Gs)

HYNOID

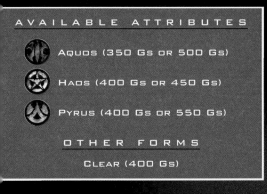

AVAILABLE ATTRIBUTES

- Aquos (350 Gs or 500 Gs)
- Haos (400 Gs or 450 Gs)
- Pyrus (400 Gs or 550 Gs)

OTHER FORMS

Clear (400 Gs)

Once Hynoid gets the scent of an enemy, it will track it down until it gets its prize. You can try to outrun this hyena-like Bakugan, but Hynoid is super fast. When it catches up to you, it will attack with a spectacular storm of thunder and lightning.

SEEN WITH: RUNO, WHO HAS A HAOS HYNOID, AND JULIE'S FRIEND BILLY, WHO HAS A SUBTERRA HYNOID.

31

JUGGERNOID

This terrifying tortoise is one of the most destructive Bakugan around. When it pounds its opponents with pure power, the shockwaves are felt all over the universe. Those who face Juggernoid have a difficult time delivering any damage. Its strong armor is nearly impossible to penetrate.

SEEN WITH: MANY BRAWLERS. DAN, RUCHO, AND MARUCHO HAVE ALL USED A JUGGERNOID IN BATTLE.

AVAILABLE ATTRIBUTES

- AQUOS (400 Gs)
- DARKUS (250 Gs or 300 Gs)
- HAOS (450 Gs)
- PYRUS (490 Gs or 540 Gs)
- SUBTERRA (450 Gs or 570 Gs)
- VENTUS (450 Gs)

LARS LION

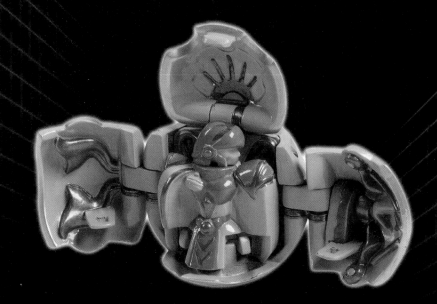

AVAILABLE ATTRIBUTES

AQUOS (500 Gs OR 600 Gs)

DARKUS (410 Gs OR 510 Gs)

HAOS (310 Gs OR 620 Gs)

SUBTERRA (540 Gs)

OTHER FORMS

DUAL ATTRIBUTE BAKUGAN
HAOS/DARKUS (540 Gs)

This shining being is the most moral of the legendary Bakugan. The armor of a knight protects her head and body from attacks. She wields a golden arrow, which she can use to bring defeated Haos Bakugan back to the field.

SEEN WITH: THE SIX LEGENDARY SOLDIERS OF VESTROIA.

LASERMAN

350G

The first thing you'll notice about this giant robot are the three enormous laser cannons on its shoulders. Each laser has a different ability. One can extinguish fire, the other can freeze water, and the third can explode rock. That means Laserman is well equipped to take down just about any Bakugan!

SEEN WITH: MASQUERADE. HE USED A DARKUS LASERMAN TO SEND BAKUGAN TO THE DOOM DIMENSION.

AVAILABLE ATTRIBUTES

- AQUOS (530 Gs)
- DARKUS (350 Gs)
- HAOS (500 Gs)
- PYRUS (400 Gs)
- VENTUS (480 Gs)

OTHER FORMS

BAKUFLIP PYRUS (470 Gs)
BAKUFLIP VENTUS (390 Gs)
DEKA AQUOS (450 Gs)
DEKA SUBTERRA (450 Gs)

LIMULUS

Limulus looks like a trilobite, an extinct sea creature with a round shell covering its body. But Limulus is a Bakugan, so it's built to attack its foes. The sharp spikes on its back keeps enemies at bay. Limulus can use the two tentacles that extend from its mouth to capture its opponents. Then it steals the strength from its enemies to make itself more powerful.

SEEN WITH: MARUCHO, WHO USED AN AQUOS LIMULUS BEFORE IT GOT SENT TO THE DOOM DIMENSION.

AVAILABLE ATTRIBUTES

- AQUOS (380 Gs, 530 Gs, OR 560 Gs)
- PYRUS (350 Gs OR 510 Gs)
- VENTUS (370 Gs OR 540 Gs)
- HAOS (440 Gs OR 550 Gs)
- VENTUS (450 Gs OR 510 Gs)

OTHER FORMS

BAKUPEARL PYRUS (480 Gs)

MANION

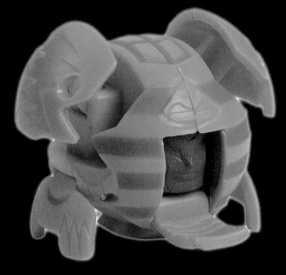

Manion resembles a sphinx from ancient Egypt, a terrifying and mysterious creature with the body of a lion, face of a human, and wings of an eagle. Golden armor protects Manion from attacks. In battle, Manion will fly above the field and then dive down to target its foe. Then it will slash at its opponent with its sharp claws.

SEEN WITH: MANY BRAWLERS. CHAN LEE USES A PYRUS MANION, AND JULIE HAS BATTLED WITH A SUBTERRA MANION.

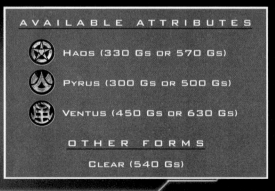

AVAILABLE ATTRIBUTES

HAOS (330 Gs or 570 Gs)

PYRUS (300 Gs or 500 Gs)

VENTUS (450 Gs or 630 Gs)

OTHER FORMS

CLEAR (540 Gs)

MANTRIS

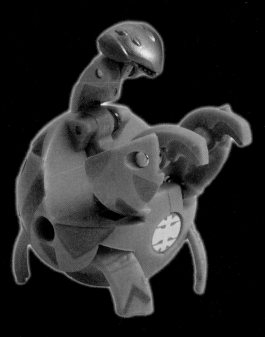

Y ou'll need more than bug spray to take down this Bakugan. Mantris has eyes in the back of its head so it can see enemies sneaking up from behind. It attacks swiftly with the sharp blades on its feet.

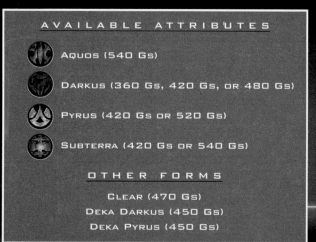

AVAILABLE ATTRIBUTES

Aquos (540 Gs)

Darkus (360 Gs, 420 Gs, or 480 Gs)

Pyrus (420 Gs or 520 Gs)

Subterra (420 Gs or 540 Gs)

OTHER FORMS

Clear (470 Gs)

Deka Darkus (450 Gs)

Deka Pyrus (450 Gs)

Seen With: Many brawlers including Masquerade, who battled with a Darkus Mantris.

MONARUS

This Bakugan looks like a beautiful butterfly, but don't be fooled by its good looks. When it flaps its wings, it can create a mighty hurricane wind to blow its opponents away! Lightweight Monarus is a super fast flyer, and it can soar right over a Gate card to escape its effects.

SEEN WITH: SHUN, WHO USES A VENTUS MONARUS IN BATTLE.

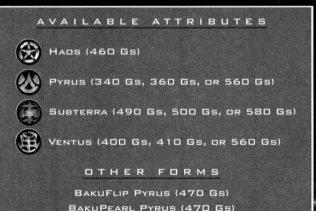

AVAILABLE ATTRIBUTES

⬟ HAOS (460 Gs)

⬟ PYRUS (340 Gs, 360 Gs, OR 560 Gs)

⬟ SUBTERRA (490 Gs, 500 Gs, OR 580 Gs)

⬟ VENTUS (400 Gs, 410 Gs, OR 560 Gs)

OTHER FORMS

BAKUFLIP PYRUS (470 Gs)
BAKUPEARL PYRUS (470 Gs)

EVOLUTION CHAIN

MONARUS

⟱

MOONLIGHT MONARUS

NAGA

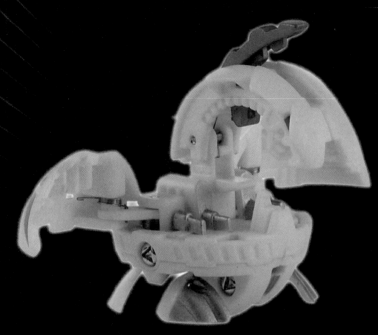

Naga looks like a skeletal dragon, which fits with his sinister personality. This Bakugan tried to steal the power from Vestroia for himself. Instead, he ended up unleashing chaos on the world of Bakugan—and things have not been right ever since.

SEEN WITH:
HAL G. NAGA USED
NEGATIVE ENERGY
TO TRANSFORM
EARTH SCIENTIST
MICHAEL INTO THE
EVIL HAL G.

AVAILABLE ATTRIBUTES

HAOS (420 Gs or 640 Gs)

PYRUS (440 Gs or 660 Gs)

SUBTERRA (450 Gs, 560 Gs, or 620 Gs)

OTHER FORMS

DUAL SUBTERRA/HAOS (450 Gs)

OBERUS

The most compassionate of the legendary Bakugan, Oberus has a beak-shaped head and a body formed by multiple butterfly wings. This Bakugan can give itself an extra boost of power to defeat an opponent—but it can only use this tactic to defeat one Bakugan at a time.

SEEN WITH: THE SIX LEGENDARY SOLDIERS OF VESTROIA.

AVAILABLE ATTRIBUTES
AQUOS (460 Gs OR 550 Gs)
SUBTERRA (490 Gs OR 570Gs)
VENTUS (420 Gs, 540 Gs, OR 670 Gs)

OTHER FORMS

DUAL HAOS/DARKUS (550 Gs)

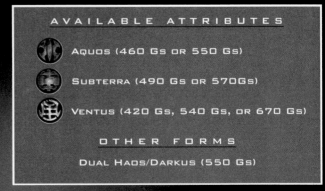

PREYAS

PREYAS IS A CORE BAKUGAN AND A SPECIAL ATTACK BAKUGAN! FOR PREYAS' INFO, FLIP TO PAGE 60 IN THE SPECIAL ATTACK SECTION.

RATTLEOID

The first thing you'll notice on this snake-like Bakugan are its glowing red eyes. Rattleoid will use them to hypnotize you—and then it will strike! Its large fangs contain a deadly poison, and its three-pronged tail lashes out like a whip. For defense, Rattleoid relies on the indestructible horns on its head, and the camouflage pattern of its scales.

SEEN WITH: JULIE AND HER FRIEND BILLY, WHO EACH HAVE USED A RATTLEOID.

AVAILABLE ATTRIBUTES

- AQUOS (340 Gs, 450 Gs, OR 490 Gs)
- DARKUS (400 Gs)
- HAOS (380 Gs OR 610 Gs)
- SUBTERRA (370 Gs, 420 Gs, 430 Gs, 540 Gs, OR 600 Gs)

OTHER FORMS

BAKUFLIP AQUOS (350 Gs)
BAKUFLIP DARKUS (390 Gs)
BAKUPEARL DARKUS (390 Gs)

RAVENOID

Ravenoid is a Bakugan that looks like a humanoid raven. It swoops down from the sky to attack its prey, grabbing it in its strong claws. Few Bakugan can escape Ravenoid's vice-like grip. Plated battle armor protects it from attacks.

SEEN WITH: SEVERAL BRAWLERS INCLUDING DAN, WHO HAS USED A PYRUS RAVENOID.

AVAILABLE ATTRIBUTES

AQUOS (570 GS)

HAOS (460 GS OR 530 GS)

PYRUS (520 GS OR 540 GS)

SUBTERRA (490 GS)

OTHER FORMS

BAKUBRONZE HAOS (600 GS)

EVOLUTION CHAIN

RAVENOID

⌄⌄

SPIN RAVENOID

REAPER

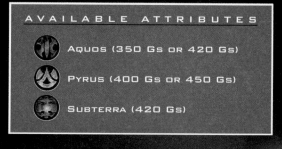

Just like the Grim Reaper of lore, Reaper carries a sharp, curved scythe that he uses to cut his opponents down to size. Reaper is fueled by rage, and his attacks are especially ferocious and cruel. You'll recognize Reaper by the horns on his head and the skeletal wings on his back.

SEEN WITH: MASQUERADE, WHO HAS BATTLED WITH A DARKUS REAPER.

AVAILABLE ATTRIBUTES

- AQUOS (350 Gs OR 420 Gs)
- PYRUS (400 Gs OR 450 Gs)
- SUBTERRA (420 Gs)

ROBOTALLIAN

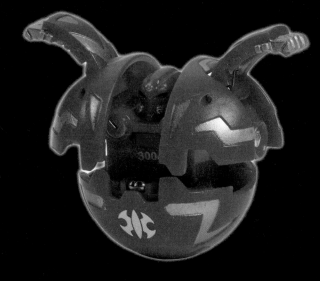

Some Bakugan are driven by anger or a lust for power, but not Robotallian. It has a strong sense of justice and will do anything to serve and protect its friends. If anything gets in its way, Robotallian will slice through it with the giant blades that extend from its body.

SEEN WITH: MANY BRAWLERS INCLUDING RUNO, WHO HAS USED A HAOS ROBOTALLIAN.

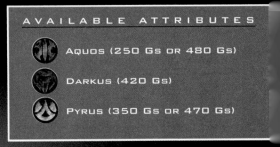

AVAILABLE ATTRIBUTES

- AQUOS (250 Gs OR 480 Gs)
- DARKUS (420 Gs)
- PYRUS (350 Gs OR 470 Gs)

SAURUS

AVAILABLE ATTRIBUTES

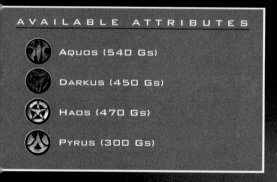

AQUOS (540 Gs)

DARKUS (450 Gs)

HAOS (470 Gs)

PYRUS (300 Gs)

Saurus is a super-tough Bakugan that looks like a dinosaur. He's short but his massive weight makes him impossible to pin down. Saurus loves to brawl, and he'll always attack an enemy head-on. When his quick temper gets the best of him, Saurus will get angry and pound the ground with his mighty fists.

SEEN WITH: SEVERAL BRAWLERS INCLUDING DAN AND RUNO.

SERPENOID

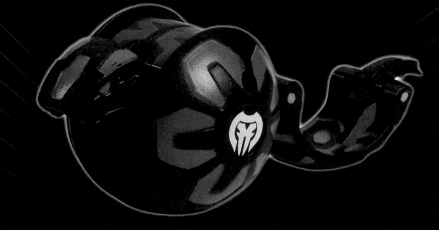

This slithering serpent moves so quickly, its foes don't see it coming. It tightly wraps its body around its enemy and then slowly, slowly drains its power.

SEEN WITH: DAN, RUNO, MARUCHO, AND JULIE, WHO HAVE ALL USED A SERPENOID IN BATTLE.

AVAILABLE ATTRIBUTES

AQUOS (450 Gs)

DARKUS (490 Gs)

HAOS (460 Gs OR 490 Gs)

SUBTERRA (350 Gs)

VENTUS (330 Gs)

OTHER FORMS

BAKUFLIP AQUOS (400 Gs)
DEKA AQUOS (450 Gs)
DEKA PYRUS (450 Gs)

SIEGE

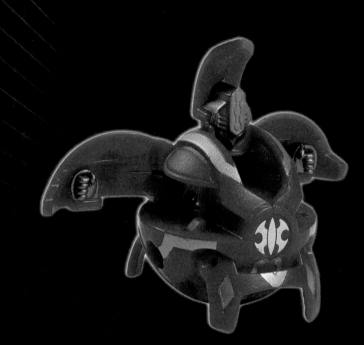

Siege looks like a knight in shining armor. He can use his cape to fly across the field or protect himself from an assault. He can change the tip of his long lance for a more effective attack on his foe.

Seen With: Several brawlers, including Masquerade, Dan, Runo, and Marucho.

SIRENOID

You won't find this mermaid-like Bakugan in any fairy tale! It's true, when Sirenoid plays her lyre it can calm the souls of everyone around. And she can use her long tail to swim gracefully through the water. But Sirenoid can also create a forceful wave that will boost her power—and destroy her opponents.

SEEN WITH: KLAUS, ONE OF MASQUERADE'S BRAWLERS. HE USES AN AQUOS SIRENOID.

AVAILABLE ATTRIBUTES

- AQUOS (370 Gs, 460 Gs, AND 630 Gs)
- DARKUS (550 Gs)
- HAOS (460 Gs)
- SUBTERRA (390 Gs OR 530 Gs)

OTHER FORMS

BAKUFLIP AQUOS

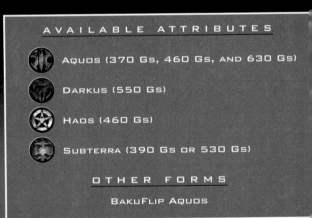

SKYRESS

SKYRESS IS A CORE BAKUGAN AND A SPECIAL ATTACK BAKUGAN! FOR SKYRESS' INFO, FLIP TO PAGE 63 IN THE SPECIAL ATTACK SECTION.

STINGLASH

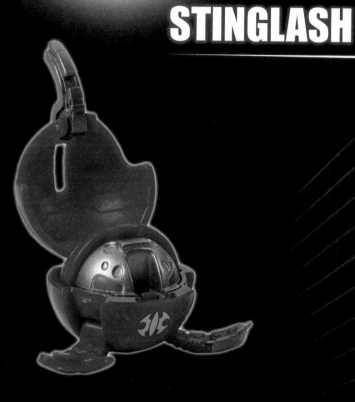

This scorpion-like Bakugan has two major methods of attack: It can slice through obstacles with its powerful pincers or poison its opponents with its sharp tail. For defense, Stinglash counts on its exoskeleton, which is made of nearly indestructible titanium steel.

SEEN WITH: MANY BRAWLERS INCLUDING DAN, WHO HAS USED A PYRUS STINGLASH, AND MARUCHO, WHO'S USED AN AQUOS STINGLASH.

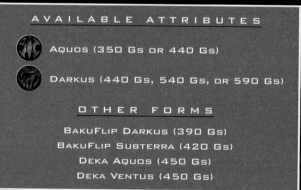

AVAILABLE ATTRIBUTES

AQUOS (350 Gs or 440 Gs)

DARKUS (440 Gs, 540 Gs, OR 590 Gs)

OTHER FORMS

BAKUFLIP DARKUS (390 Gs)
BAKUFLIP SUBTERRA (420 Gs)
DEKA AQUOS (450 Gs)
DEKA VENTUS (450 Gs)

STORM SKYRESS

When Skyress evolves, she becomes larger and stronger. Storm Skyress has wings that span the battlefield. One of her long tail feathers is tipped with a sharp, curved blade.

Like Skyress, Storm Skyress fights for what's right. Storm Skyress was captured by the Vexos and later freed. She decided to stay in New Vestroia to watch over it and keep it safe.

SEEN WITH: SHUN, WHOSE VENTUS SKYRESS EVOLVED INTO STORM SKYRESS WHEN HE REALIZED HE NEEDED THE HELP OF HIS FRIENDS.

AVAILABLE ATTRIBUTES

AQUOS (320 Gs or 440 Gs)

HAOS (350 Gs or 480 Gs)

SUBTERRA (550Gs)

VENTUS (500 Gs or 650 Gs)

OTHER FORMS

BAKULYTE AQUOS (600 Gs)
BAKULYTE VENTUS (600 Gs)
BAKUBRONZE (630 Gs)

EVOLUTION
CHAIN

SKYRESS

STORM SKYRESS

TENTACLEAR

This Bakugan has its eye on you! It's one giant eyeball with six tentacles around it. The eyeball can emit a shining beam of light to blind its enemy. And each of the tentacles can deliver a sharp sting.

SEEN WITH: JULIO, ONE OF MASQUERADE'S BRAWLERS. HE USED A HAOS TENTACLEAR IN BATTLE.

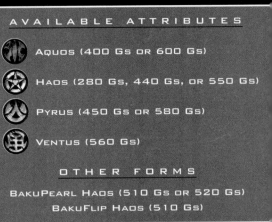

AVAILABLE ATTRIBUTES

- AQUOS (400 GS OR 600 GS)
- HAOS (280 GS, 440 GS, OR 550 GS)
- PYRUS (450 GS OR 580 GS)
- VENTUS (560 GS)

OTHER FORMS

BAKUPEARL HAOS (510 GS OR 520 GS)
BAKUFLIP HAOS (510 GS)

TERRORCLAW

AVAILABLE ATTRIBUTES

- AQUOS (330 Gs OR 450 Gs)
- PYRUS (360 Gs OR 540 Gs)
- SUBTERRA (420 Gs OR 660 Gs)
- VENTUS (540 Gs)

OTHER FORMS

BakuFlip Haos (450 Gs)
BakuFlip Subterra (470 Gs)
Clear (450 Gs)
Deka Aquos (450 Gs)
Deka Subterra (450 Gs)

Thanks to its six legs, Terrorclaw is one of the fastest Bakugan around. Of course, its legs aren't what make this monster dangerous. It's its terrifying claws, of course! They can really put a squeeze on Terrorclaw's enemies.

TIGRERRA

Tigrerra's ferocious nature makes her a dangerous foe on the field. She's also fiercely loyal to her battle partner, and has a strong sense of what's right and wrong. Besides using her razor-sharp claws and teeth, Tigrerra can attack with a large blade inside her body that can slice any substance in the human world.

SEEN WITH: RUNO, WHOSE GUARDIAN BAKUGAN WAS A HAOS TIGRERRA BEFORE SHE EVOLVED.

AVAILABLE ATTRIBUTES

AQUOS (450 Gs)

DARKUS (480 Gs)

HAOS (350 Gs, 450 Gs, 510 Gs, or 610 Gs)

PYRUS (520 Gs)

VENTUS (450 Gs, 500 Gs, or 530 Gs)

OTHER FORMS

CLEAR (580 Gs)

FOR EVOLUTION CHAIN, FLIP TO PAGE 12.

TUSKOR

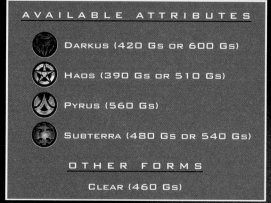

AVAILABLE ATTRIBUTES

- DARKUS (420 Gs OR 600 Gs)
- HAOS (390 Gs OR 510 Gs)
- PYRUS (560 Gs)
- SUBTERRA (480 Gs OR 540 Gs)

OTHER FORMS

CLEAR (460 Gs)

This massive mammoth-like Bakugan has dangerous spikes on the end of its long trunk. It uses its trunk as a weapon to smash its foes. Tuskor can also attack with her four huge tusks, which can penetrate any armor.

SEEN WITH: MANY BRAWLERS INCLUDING DAN, RUNO, JULIE, AND BILLY.

WARIUS

This ogre-like warrior loves to brawl, and it's built to deliver damage. It pounds foes with a giant mace studded with spikes. Its own body is protected by horns, spikes, and thick plates of armor.

SEEN WITH: MANY BRAWLERS INCLUDING DAN AND CHAN LEE.

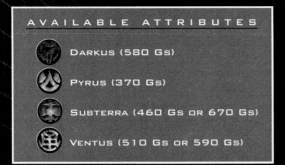

AVAILABLE ATTRIBUTES

DARKUS (580 Gs)

PYRUS (370 Gs)

SUBTERRA (460 Gs OR 670 Gs)

VENTUS (510 Gs OR 590 Gs)

WAVERN

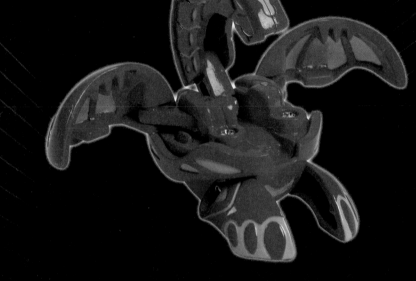

Wavern is Naga's twin sister, but she's the complete opposite of her evil brother. When Naga tried to steal the power of Vestroia she held the Infinity Core inside her, protecting Vestroia's positive power source. This made her nearly impossible to defeat. The more negative energy aimed at her, the stronger she became.

SEEN WITH: JOE, THE WEBMASTER OF THE BAKUGAN WEB SITE, AND HER GOOD FRIEND DRAGO.

AVAILABLE ATTRIBUTES

DARKUS (440 GS OR 580 GS)

HAOS (370 GS OR 600 GS)

VENTUS (360 GS OR 560 GS)

OTHER FORMS

DUAL ATTRIBUTE BAKUGAN
AQUOS/VENTUS (600 GS)

WORMQUAKE

What do you get when you cross a worm with an earthqake? A giant Bakugan that can really shake up a battle! Its mouth contains rows of terrifying teeth to tear through anything in its path. It can travel underground and then burst through the earth to surprise its foes. Then it squeezes them with the curved spikes on its body.

SEEN WITH: SEVERAL BRAWLERS, INCLUDING JULIE'S FRIEND BILLY, WHO USES A SUBTERRA WORMQUAKE.

AVAILABLE ATTRIBUTES

- HAOS (440 GS OR 500 GS)
- SUBTERRA (400 GS)
- VENTUS (550 GS)

OTHER FORMS

DARKUS (440 GS OR 580 GS)
HAOS (370 GS OR 600 GS)
VENTUS (360 GS OR 560 GS)

PREYAS

On the field, Preyas is a regular comedy act, making jokes and razzing his opponents. But his battle style is serious. This chameleon can change his molecular structure to become any one of the six attributes. That means he can take whatever his opponents dish out!

SEEN WITH: MARUCHO, WHOSE FIRST GUARDIAN BAKUGAN WAS PREYAS.

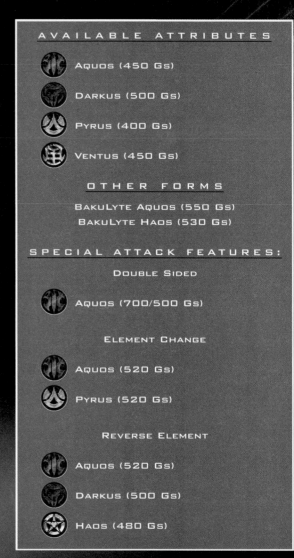

AVAILABLE ATTRIBUTES

- AQUOS (450 Gs)
- DARKUS (500 Gs)
- PYRUS (400 Gs)
- VENTUS (450 Gs)

OTHER FORMS

BAKULYTE AQUOS (550 Gs)
BAKULYTE HAOS (530 Gs)

SPECIAL ATTACK FEATURES:

DOUBLE SIDED

- AQUOS (700/500 Gs)

ELEMENT CHANGE

- AQUOS (520 Gs)
- PYRUS (520 Gs)

REVERSE ELEMENT

- AQUOS (520 Gs)
- DARKUS (500 Gs)
- HAOS (480 Gs)

EVOLUTION CHAIN

PREYAS

PREYAS II
(PREYAS ANGELO +
PREYAS DIABLO)

61

PREYAS II

A Preyas egg hatched, and two brothers emerged: one good, and one evil. Preyas Angelo is the good brother. On the field, he shines like a bright angel. His large, feathery wings and the smaller wings on his arms and legs give him the power of flight.

Preyas Angelo may look like an angel, but his brother Preyas Diablo looks quite devilish. His wings are spiked and leathery, he's got horns on his head, and vampire-like fangs. He uses his Preyas energy to dole out fiery punishment to his foes.

SEEN WITH:
MARUCHO.

AVAILABLE ATTRIBUTES

Aquos (500 Gs)

Subterra (480 Gs or 520 Gs)

OTHER FORMS

BakuBronze Aquos (630 Gs),
BakuLyte Aquos (590 Gs), BakuLyte Haos (600 Gs),
BakuPearl Aquos (580 Gs)

SPECIAL ATTACK FEATURE:

G-Power Spinner (One of three possible G-Powers
listed is randomly generated on each roll)

Aquos: 660 – 540 – 400 Gs

Darkus: 680 – 360 – 550 Gs

Haos: 670 – 380 – 530 Gs

Pyrus: 670 – 420 – 530 Gs

Subterra: 670 – 380 – 570 Gs

Ventus: 660 – 450 – 520 Gs

FOR EVOLUTION CHAIN, FLIP TO PAGE 61.

SKYRESS

This Bakugan's amazing powers match her magnificent appearance. She's a huge bird with long, beautiful wings and sharp-edged tail feathers. She believes in battling fair, but that doesn't mean she's easy to beat. Skyress has incredible vision for locating her foes. If she is defeated, she can return to the field like a phoenix rising from the ashes.

SEEN WITH: SHUN, WHO HAD A VENTUS SKYRESS AS HIS GUARDIAN BAKUGAN.

AVAILABLE ATTRIBUTES

- DARKUS (490 Gs)
- PYRUS (350 Gs or 370 Gs)
- SUBTERRA (500 Gs)
- VENTUS (450 Gs or 550 Gs)

OTHER FORMS

BAKULYTE AQUOS (530 Gs)
BAKULYTE VENTUS (510 Gs)
BAKUPEARL SUBTERRA (550 Gs)

SPECIAL ATTACK FEATURE:

REVERSE ELEMENT

- AQUOS (540 Gs)
- SUBTERRA (550 Gs)
- VENTUS (540 Gs)

FOR EVOLUTION CHAIN, FLIP TO PAGE 51.

NEW VESTROIA

Naga and Hal G nearly destroyed Vestroia, but thanks to Wavern and Drago the six worlds combined to become one new, beautiful world: New Vestroia. Bakugan lived together in peace and harmony. But those peaceful times didn't last long.

The Vestals invaded, capturing and enslaving the Bakugan and battling them for sport. They also brought with them their own technology, and the first mechanical Bakugan were created. And brawlers on New Vestroia saw Bakugan Traps for the first time—Bakugan that can battle on their own as well as combine with other Bakugan to form bigger, better monsters.

ABISOMEGA

This Bakugan is built like a sea serpent, with a long, snake-like body and three fins for swimming. Abisomega can live in both fresh and saltwater, blending into its surroundings thanks to the diamond pattern on its body. Because of its flexible shape, it can attack quickly and efficiently.

SEEN WITH: MYLENE, A VEXOS BRAWLER FROM NEW VESTROIA. SHE RESURRECTED THIS EXTINCT BAKUGAN AS AN ENERGY BODY.

AVAILABLE ATTRIBUTES

- AQUOS (610 Gs, 660 Gs, OR 670 Gs)
- HAOS (550 Gs OR 750 Gs)
- PYRUS (530 Gs, 650 Gs, OR 730 Gs)
- SUBTERRA (560 Gs, 660 Gs, OR 680 Gs)
- VENTUS (540 Gs)

OTHER FORMS

BAKULYTE PYRUS (750 Gs)

ALPHA PERCIVAL

EVOLUTION CHAIN

PERCIVAL

MIDNIGHT PERCIVAL

ALPHA PERCIVAL

PERCIVAL VORTEX

ALPHA PERCIVAL CYCLONE

When this Bakugan evolves from Midnight Percival, he gets a new cape that grants him extra abilities. He can hover in the air to position an attack over his prey. With his double-ended sword, he can take on more than one attacker at a time.

SEEN WITH: ACE OF THE BAKUGAN RESISTANCE.

AVAILABLE ATTRIBUTES

 DARKUS (520 Gs, 550 Gs, 600 Gs, OR 720 Gs)

PYRUS (500 Gs)

SUBTERRA (600 Gs)

VENTUS (510 Gs OR 630 Gs)

OTHER FORMS

DEKA DARKUS (640 Gs)

ALTAIR

Altair is the first mechanical Bakugan ever created. Professor Clay on New Vestroia built Altair and loaded it with impressive attack abilities. It can slash opponents with its sharp fangs and horns. It can fly swiftly with its wings or hover in mid-air. Red lenses in its eyes allow it to see—and attack—at night. In battle, Altair can shoot a hot blast of white steam from its mouth.

SEEN WITH: VEXOS BRAWLER LYNC, WHO USES IT TO BATTLE THE RESISTANCE ON NEW VESTROIA.

AVAILABLE ATTRIBUTES

- AQUOS (610 Gs)
- HAOS (520 Gs, 650 Gs, OR 720 Gs)
- PYRUS (670 Gs OR 700 Gs)
- VENTUS (500 Gs, 630 Gs, OR 710 Gs)

OTHER FORMS

BAKUFROST DARKUS (730 Gs)
BAKUFROST HAOS (550 Gs OR 740 Gs)
BAKULYTE VENTUS (640 Gs)
BAKUSOLAR DARKUS (550 Gs OR 610 Gs)

ALTO BRONTES

BRONTES

MEGA BRONTES

ALTO BRONTES

Alto Brontes has a bad attitude! The more opponents he defeats, the meaner this Bakugan gets. An extra set of arms helps him take down multiple foes at once. This big, bad Bakugan is ten times stronger than his Mega Brontes form. That's a good thing, but what Alto Brontes gains in strength he loses in speed.

SEEN WITH: VEXOS BRAWLER GUS GRAV, WHO EVOLVED HIS MEGA BRONTES DURING A BATTLE.

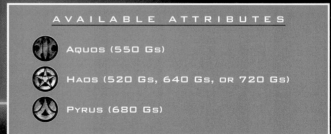

AVAILABLE ATTRIBUTES

Aquos (550 Gs)

Haos (520 Gs, 640 Gs, or 720 Gs)

Pyrus (680 Gs)

68

ATMOS

The wings on this falcon-like mechanical Bakugan are the largest of any Bakugan. These record-breaking wings do double duty. They allow Atmos to fly and attack with amazing speed. Then Atmos can lash out at its opponent with the wing's deadly blades. A sharp beak, horn, and clawed feet help Atmos finish the job.

SEEN WITH: VEXOS BRAWLER LYNC VOLAN—UNTIL DAN DEFEATED LYNC IN BATTLE AND CLAIMED ATMOS FOR HIS OWN.

AVAILABLE ATTRIBUTES

AQUOS (570 GS OR 750 GS)

PYRUS (650 GS)

SUBTERRA (540 GS)

OTHER FORMS

BAKULYTE AQUOS (720 GS)
BAKUFLIP AQUOS (680 GS)

BRONTES

Like Altair, Brontes is a mechanical Bakugan with a monstrous size. Even though it's large, it's fast. It can fly using the propeller on its head, and jump with its long legs to avoid an enemy attack. During battle, Brontes will stretch out its long arms and wrap them around an opponent.

SEEN WITH: VEXOS BRAWLER VOLT, BATTLING AGAINST THE RESISTANCE.

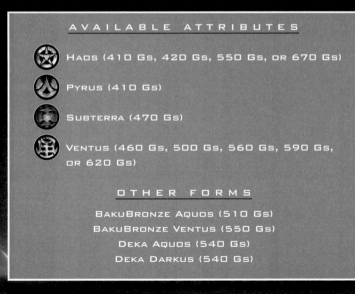

AVAILABLE ATTRIBUTES

HAOS (410 GS, 420 GS, 550 GS, OR 670 GS)

PYRUS (410 GS)

SUBTERRA (470 GS)

VENTUS (460 GS, 500 GS, 560 GS, 590 GS, OR 620 GS)

OTHER FORMS

BAKUBRONZE AQUOS (510 GS)
BAKUBRONZE VENTUS (550 GS)
DEKA AQUOS (540 GS)
DEKA DARKUS (540 GS)

FOR EVOLUTION CHAIN, FLIP TO PAGE 68.

COSMIC INGRAM

EVOLUTION CHAIN

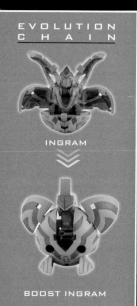

INGRAM

BOOST INGRAM

COSMIC INGRAM

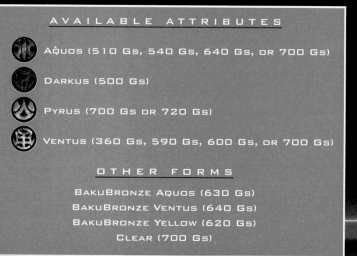

Cosmic Ingram is like an armored bird of prey. It can pinpoint the location of its enemies with its glowing red eyes. This flying Bakugan has an impressive six wings. Its feathers are metal plates that can protect its body from attacks, including fire.

AVAILABLE ATTRIBUTES

- AQUOS (510 Gs, 540 Gs, 640 Gs, OR 700 Gs)
- DARKUS (500 Gs)
- PYRUS (700 Gs OR 720 Gs)
- VENTUS (360 Gs, 590 Gs, 600 Gs, OR 700 Gs)

OTHER FORMS

BAKUBRONZE AQUOS (630 Gs)
BAKUBRONZE VENTUS (640 Gs)
BAKUBRONZE YELLOW (620 Gs)
CLEAR (700 Gs)

DUAL ELFIN

EVOLUTION
CHAIN

ELFIN

DUAL ELFIN

DUAL ELFIN
REVOLUTION

Dual Elfin is a good Bakugan at heart who protects helpless Bakugan on New Vestroia. She has an amazing ability—she can battle using two attributes at the same time.

SEEN WITH: PREYAS, HER GOOD FRIEND.

AVAILABLE ATTRIBUTES

 Aquos (510 Gs, 520 Gs, 690 Gs, or 700 Gs)

Pyrus (640 Gs or 750 Gs)

Haos (500 Gs or 520 Gs)

Ventus (550 Gs)

OTHER FORMS

BakuFrost Subterra (600 Gs)
BakuSolar Haos (600 Gs)
BakuBronze Aquos (640 Gs)
BakuLyte Pyrus (540 Gs)
Deka Aquos (580 Gs)

FENCER

Fencer is one of the mechanical Bakugan created by the Vestals of New Vestroia. It's built for battle, with sharp blades on its front legs and a long, whip-like tail with a blaster on the end. It can grip enemies with its strong pincers. Fast-moving Fencer can also stun opponents during battle with a blast from its eye. It can combine with six other Bakugan to become the Special Attack Bakugan Maxus Helios.

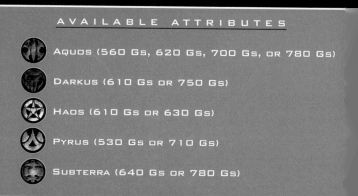

AVAILABLE ATTRIBUTES

- AQUOS (560 Gs, 620 Gs, 700 Gs, OR 780 Gs)
- DARKUS (610 Gs OR 750 Gs)
- HAOS (610 Gs OR 630 Gs)
- PYRUS (530 Gs OR 710 Gs)
- SUBTERRA (640 Gs OR 780 Gs)

FOXBAT

This mechanical Bakugan's wings can be used for both offense and defense. It can fly quickly and at great heights, and it can also wrap its wings around its body for protection. Foxbat's claws are also useful—they're sharp enough to tear through armor. And while Foxbat may have poor vision during the day, it can pinpoint any target using its night vision. Foxbat can combine with six other Bakugan to form the Special Attack Bakugan Maxus Helios.

SEEN WITH:
VEXOS
BRAWLER
SPECTRA
PHANTOM.

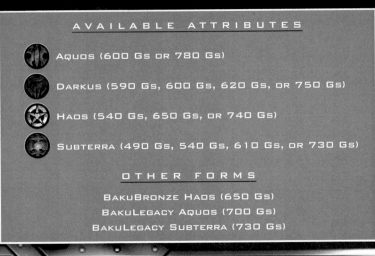

AVAILABLE ATTRIBUTES

AQUOS (600 Gs or 780 Gs)

DARKUS (590 Gs, 600 Gs, 620 Gs, or 750 Gs)

HAOS (540 Gs, 650 Gs, or 740 Gs)

SUBTERRA (490 Gs, 540 Gs, 610 Gs, or 730 Gs)

OTHER FORMS

BAKUBRONZE HAOS (650 Gs)
BAKULEGACY AQUOS (700 Gs)
BAKULEGACY SUBTERRA (730 Gs)

FR

...d spins around, so it can see attackers from every directic
...s large brain is protected by a glass case. And it has a can
...so it can blast away at its enemies. While Freezer's head
...ght be even cooler. If one of them is damaged, a new one

...VEXOS BRAWLER VOLT LUSTER, WHO LOST HIS
...A BATTLE WITH DAN.

AVAILABLE ATTRIBUTES

- DARKUS (500 Gs, 660 Gs, or 760 Gs)
- PYRUS (740 Gs)
- VENTUS (700 Gs)

HADES

EVOLUTION
CHAIN

HADES

MYRIAD HADES

TURBINE HADES

What's scarier than a three-headed Dragonoid? How about one that's completely covered in impenetrable armor! This mechanical monster can shoot fire from each of its heads. It can swiftly soar with its six wings. Hades can use its three spike-tipped tails to assault multiple foes. This powerhouse is almost impossible to take down. Even its heart is protected by three large metal thorns!

SEEN WITH:
SHADOW, A
VEXOS BRAWLER.
HADES WAS
CREATED BY
PROFESSOR
CLAY TO BATTLE
THE BAKUGAN
RESISTANCE.

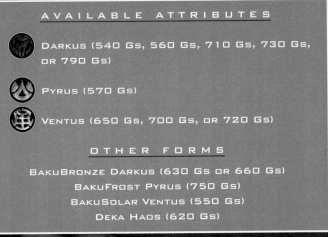

AVAILABLE ATTRIBUTES

DARKUS (540 Gs, 560 Gs, 710 Gs, 730 Gs, OR 790 Gs)

PYRUS (570 Gs)

VENTUS (650 Gs, 700 Gs, OR 720 Gs)

OTHER FORMS

BAKUBRONZE DARKUS (630 Gs OR 660 Gs)
BAKUFROST PYRUS (750 Gs)
BAKUSOLAR VENTUS (550 Gs)
DEKA HAOS (620 Gs)

HELIOS

EVOLUTION CHAIN

HELIOS

VIPER HELIOS

TURBINE HELIOS

MAXUS HELIOS

ORBIT HELIOS

is dragon-like Bakugan has an evil streak as sharp as the
oison-tipped thorns that stick out of its body. Like most winged
ugan, Helios can fly swiftly above the battlefield to avoid—or
et—its opponent. Then it barrages its foe with cannonball
ts of fire from its mouth. Helios becomes stronger when it
bines with other Bakugan to form Maxus Helios.

EN WITH: VESTOS BRAWLER SPECTRA PHANTOM.

AVAILABLE ATTRIBUTES

AQUOS (460 GS OR 660 GS)

DARKUS (500 GS, 520 GS, 650 GS, OR 750 GS)

HAOS (580 GS, 630 GS, OR 770 GS)

PYRUS (450 GS, 600 GS, 620 GS, 650 GS, OR 680 GS)

SUBTERRA (540 GS, 600 GS, OR 780 GS)

VENTUS (500 GS, 590 GS, 700 GS, OR 780 GS)

OTHER FORMS

BAKUBRONZE PYRUS (600 GS OR 660 GS)
BAKUEXOSKIN DARKUS (700 GS)
BAKUMUTATION AQUOS (720 OR 780 GS)
BAKUMUTATION PYRUS (560 OR 600 GS)
DEKA PYRUS (640 GS)

HYDRANOID

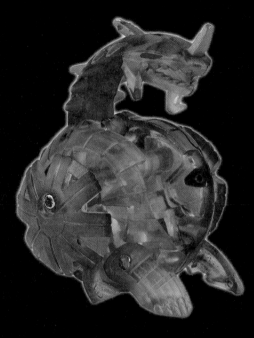

Hydranoid's unevolved form is tough, too. The special cell structure of this Bakugan makes it difficult to injure in battle, and its fighting abilities make for a formidable attack. Hydranoid's long, spiked tail has sent more than one foe to the Doom Dimension!

SEEN WITH: MASQUERADE.

AVAILABLE ATTRIBUTES

BAKULYTE DARKUS 450 GS

FOR EVOLUTION CHAIN, FLIP TO PAGE 18.

HYPER DRAGONOID

Every Dragonoid form has qualities that separate it from the other evolved forms. Hyper Dragonoid shoots fire balls from its mouth, but these fire balls can split in two to attack multiple opponents. It's sleeker and more agile than its pre-evolved form, Pyro Dragonoid. It can move the horns on its head in any direction for greater attack and defense power. And Hyper Dragonoid has one more unique ability: It can blend into its surroundings and then launch a sneak attack.

AVAILABLE ATTRIBUTES

- DARKUS (530 Gs OR 730 Gs)
- HAOS (580 Gs OR 740 Gs)
- PYRUS (500 Gs, 560 Gs, 600 Gs, 740 Gs, OR 800 Gs)
- SUBTERRA (700 Gs, 720 Gs, OR 780 Gs)
- VENTUS (550 Gs)

OTHER FORMS

BAKULEGACY DARKUS (730 Gs)
BAKULEGACY HAOS (730 Gs)
BAKULYTE DARKUS (670 Gs)
BAKUMUTATION AQUOS (530 Gs OR 600 Gs)
BAKUMUTATION DARKUS (690 Gs OR 760 Gs)
BAKUMUTATION PYRUS (580 Gs, 620 Gs, 720 Gs, OR 780 Gs)
CLEAR (740 Gs)

FOR EVOLUTION CHAIN, FLIP TO PAGE 17.

INGRAM

Ingram can fly high into the sky with its six wings, and then dive down to earth to target prey. Then he shreds his opponents with his razor-sharp claws. When Ingram is attacked it's protected by its steel-plated chest. To increase this Bakugan's power, you can combine it with Trap Bakugan Hylash.

SEEN WITH:
SHUN.
VENTUS INGRAM
BECOMES HIS
GUARDIAN
BAKUGAN
AFTER HE IS
SEPARATED
FROM SKYRESS.

AVAILABLE ATTRIBUTES

AQUOS (510 Gs, 660 Gs, or 750 Gs)

DARKUS (510 Gs, 610 Gs, 730 Gs, or 790 Gs)

HAOS (730 Gs or 770 Gs)

PYRUS (670 Gs or 710 Gs)

SUBTERRA (450 Gs or 650 Gs)

VENTUS (430 Gs, 460 Gs, 650 Gs, 670 Gs, or 780 Gs)

OTHER FORMS

BAKULEGACY AQUOS (700 Gs)
BAKULEGACY PYRUS (720 Gs), BAKULYTE AQUOS (640 Gs)
BAKULYTE SUBTERRA (670 Gs), BAKULYTE VENTUS (650 Gs)
BAKUMUTATION HAOS/CLEAR (660 Gs or 760 Gs)
BAKUMUTATION SUBTERRA (550 Gs or 600 Gs)

FOR EVOLUTION CHAIN, FLIP TO PAGE 71.

KLAWGOR

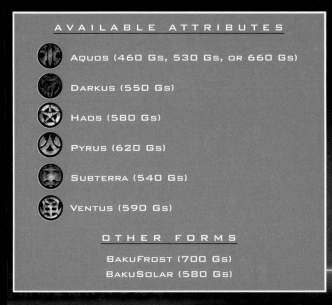

Klawgor may be small, but this Bakugan has many tricks it can use to take down a foe. It can open up to reveal multiple layers of attack hardware, including sharp spikes, pincers, and a tail that can blast opponents with deadly firepower. Klawgor becomes even stronger when it combines with other Bakugan to form Maxus Helios, a Special Attack Bakugan.

AVAILABLE ATTRIBUTES

- AQUOS (460 Gs, 530 Gs, OR 660 Gs)
- DARKUS (550 Gs)
- HAOS (580 Gs)
- PYRUS (620 Gs)
- SUBTERRA (540 Gs)
- VENTUS (590 Gs)

OTHER FORMS

BakuFrost (700 Gs)
BakuSolar (580 Gs)

LEEFRAM

This Bakugan looks like a robotic snake, but it's packed with extras that make it far more dangerous than any serpent. Leefram has two arms with curved blades on the ends, a deadly sharp horn on top of its head, and fangs loaded with venom. Its snake-like shape allows Leefram to stand tall on the battlefield—the perfect position to make quick and deadly strikes. Leefram can combine with other Bakugan to form the Special Attack Bakugan Maxus Helios.

AVAILABLE ATTRIBUTES

Aquos (570 Gs or 590 Gs)

Darkus (500 Gs or 650 Gs)

Subterra (600 Gs)

Ventus (490 Gs)

OTHER FORMS

BakuMutation Darkus (560 Gs, 570 Gs, 580 Gs, 680 Gs, or 750 Gs)

BakuMutation Ventus (570 Gs, 580 Gs, or 620 Gs)

MEGA BR

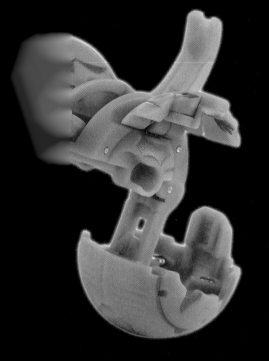

When Bron
Mega Br
in size. Mega
for defense. I
can withstand
and it can elu
amazing spee
the attack, M
squeeze its fo
grip.

SEEN WITH
BRAWLER V

AVAILABLE ATTRIBUTES

AQUOS (580 GS)

DARKUS (660 GS)

HAOS (600 GS, 640 GS, OR 700 GS)

SUBTERRA (550 GS)

VENTUS (550 GS)

OTHER FORMS

BAKULYTE HAOS (600 GS)

FOR EVOLUTION CHAIN, FLIP TO PAGE 68.

MEGA NEMUS

Mega Nemus wears a crown of gold, but it's not for decoration. Embedded in the crown are four stones with incredibly destructive power. This Bakugan can also use a spear to launch two disks at its enemies. It also has great defenses: Its extra armor protects it from fire, wind, and water.

SEEN WITH: BARON OF THE BAKUGAN RESISTANCE.

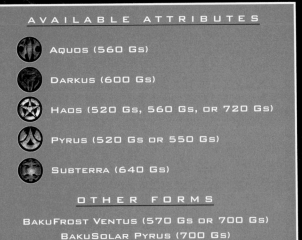

AVAILABLE ATTRIBUTES

- AQUOS (560 Gs)
- DARKUS (600 Gs)
- HAOS (520 Gs, 560 Gs, OR 720 Gs)
- PYRUS (520 Gs OR 550 Gs)
- SUBTERRA (640 Gs)

OTHER FORMS

BAKUFROST VENTUS (570 Gs OR 700 Gs)
BAKUSOLAR PYRUS (700 Gs)
DEKA HAOS (640 Gs)

EVOLUTION CHAIN

NEMUS

⌄⌄

MEGA NEMUS

MIDNIGHT PERCIVAL

When you face Midnight Percival on the battlefield, you'll need to watch out for his steel sword—and the fire-breathing dragon heads he has on each shoulder! Getting through his defenses isn't easy.

He's got strong armor, horns on his head and shoulders, and a cape that shields him from fire and water.

SEEN WITH: ACE OF THE BAKUGAN RESISTANCE.

AVAILABLE ATTRIBUTES

AQUOS (580 Gs)

DARKUS (610 Gs)

HAOS (550 Gs OR 570 Gs)

OTHER FORMS

TRANSLUCENT DARKUS (700 Gs)

FOR EVOLUTION CHAIN, FLIP TO PAGE 66.

MOSK

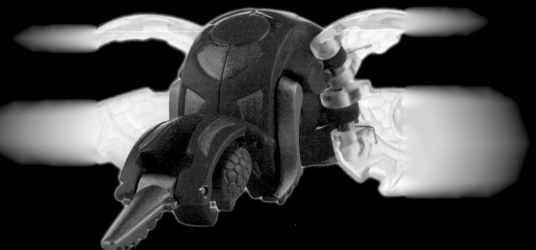

Bakugan is no backyard pest. It's loaded with lots of sha
tacks: a compact but deadly stinger; a sharp spear on th
ws; and lethal barbs all over its body. Fast-flying Moskee
excellent sight.

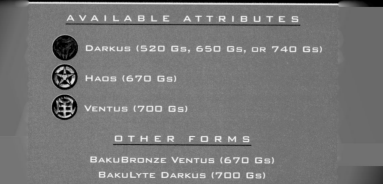

AVAILABLE ATTRIBUTES

- DARKUS (520 Gs, 650 Gs, OR 740 Gs)
- HAOS (670 Gs)
- VENTUS (700 Gs)

OTHER FORMS

BAKUBRONZE VENTUS (670 Gs)
BAKULYTE DARKUS (700 Gs)

IAD HADES

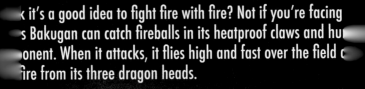

k it's a good idea to fight fire with fire? Not if you're facing
s Bakugan can catch fireballs in its heatproof claws and hu
onent. When it attacks, it flies high and fast over the field c
ire from its three dragon heads.

SHADOW, A VEXOS BRAWLER.

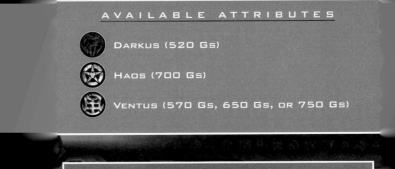

AVAILABLE ATTRIBUTES

DARKUS (520 GS)

HAOS (700 GS)

VENTUS (570 GS, 650 GS, OR 750 GS)

FOR EVOLUTION CHAIN, FLIP TO PAGE 76.

NEMUS

Nemus is a commanding figure on the field. He looks like an ancient Egyptian king with with massive blade-like wings of gold. The bands on his wrists can deflect enemy attacks, and the tall cane he carries can shoot out a destructive beam of light.

SEEN WITH:
BARON OF THE
BAKUGAN
RESISTANCE,
WHO HAS A
HAOS NEMUS.

AVAILABLE ATTRIBUTES

- AQUOS (580 Gs)
- DARKUS (400 Gs OR 560 Gs)
- HAOS (450 Gs, 470 Gs, 500 Gs, 520 Gs, 630 Gs, AND 720 Gs)
- PYRUS (520 Gs)
- SUBTERRA (640 Gs)

OTHER FORMS

BAKUBRONZE VENTUS (600 Gs)
BAKUBRONZE YELLOW (530 Gs)
BAKULYTE HAOS (505 Gs)
DEKA HAOS (540 Gs), DEKA VENTUS (540 Gs)

FOR EVOLUTION CHAIN, FLIP TO PAGE 84.

NEO DRAGONOID

Neo Dragonoid's most amazing feature is his impossibly large wings. They act as a shield against fire, water, and wind. Drago had become part of Vestroia's Perfect Core before the Six Legendary Soldiers freed him. He had to leave some of his energy with the Perfect Core, so this form is less powerful in some ways than his previous evolved forms.

This Bakugan also has one other amazing ability. It can combine with six Trap Bakugan to form the mighty Maxus Dragonoid.

SEEN WITH: DAN KUSO. DRAGO EVOLVED INTO NEO DRAGONOID AFTER HE AND THE OTHER SIX FIGHTING BAKUGAN SAVED VESTROIA FROM DESTRUCTION AND RESURRECTED NEW VESTROIA.

AVAILABLE ATTRIBUTES

 AQUOS (490 Gs, 540 Gs, 620 Gs, or 750 Gs)

DARKUS (480 Gs, 490 Gs, 530 Gs, 575 Gs, 640 Gs, or 700 Gs)

 HAOS (500 Gs, 550 Gs, 560 Gs, or 730 Gs)

 PYRUS (410 Gs, 460 Gs, 520 Gs, 550 Gs, 560 Gs, 580 Gs, 610 Gs, 630 Gs, 650 Gs, 680 Gs, 710 Gs, or 740 Gs)

 SUBTERRA (500 Gs, 560 Gs, 720 Gs, or 750 Gs)

VENTUS (460 Gs)

OTHER FORMS

BAKUBRONZE PYRUS (640 Gs or 650 Gs), BAKULEGACY AQUOS (750 Gs)
BAKULEGACY PYRUS (700 Gs), BAKULYTE DARKUS (510 Gs or 610 Gs)
BAKULYTE PYRUS (500 Gs or 610 Gs), BAKULYTE SUBTERRA (600 Gs)
DEKA AQUOS (540 Gs), DEKA HAOS (580 Gs)
DEKA PYRUS (540 Gs or 580 Gs), DEKA VENTUS (540 Gs)

FOR EVOLUTION CHAIN, FLIP TO PAGE 17.

PERCIVAL

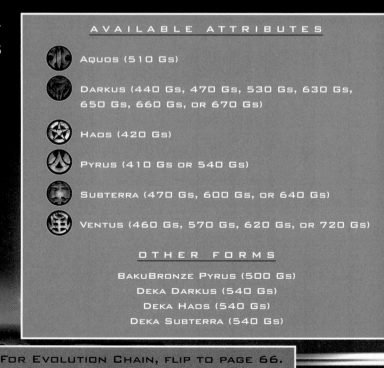

Percival has enough amazing features to rival any superhero. He can use his cape to turn invisible and then launch plasma bullets from one of his three mouths. His body is protected by unbreakable horns on his head and shoulders; armor made of steel; and two dragon head wrist guards. And that's not all—Percival can create a black tornado to devastate his challenger!

SEEN WITH: ACE OF THE BAKUGAN RESISTANCE, WHO HAS A DARKUS PERCIVAL.

AVAILABLE ATTRIBUTES

AQUOS (510 Gs)

DARKUS (440 Gs, 470 Gs, 530 Gs, 630 Gs, 650 Gs, 660 Gs, OR 670 Gs)

HAOS (420 Gs)

PYRUS (410 Gs OR 540 Gs)

SUBTERRA (470 Gs, 600 Gs, OR 640 Gs)

VENTUS (460 Gs, 570 Gs, 620 Gs, OR 720 Gs)

OTHER FORMS

BAKUBRONZE PYRUS (500 Gs)
DEKA DARKUS (540 Gs)
DEKA HAOS (540 Gs)
DEKA SUBTERRA (540 Gs)

FOR EVOLUTION CHAIN, FLIP TO PAGE 66.

PYRO DRAGONOID

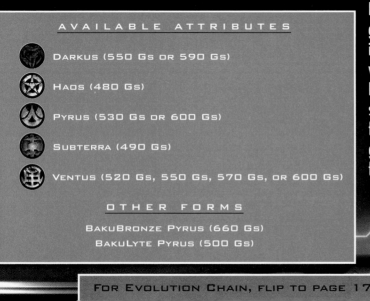

530ɢ

When Neo Dragonoid evolves into Pyro Dragonoid, it grows extra wings to give it extra speed. The golden tips on its wings can deflect enemy attacks. If Pyro Dragonoid does get hit and loses its tail, the tail will regrow. This Bakugan can also shoot fiery blasts from the golden gem on its forehead.

AVAILABLE ATTRIBUTES

DARKUS (550 Gs or 590 Gs)

HAOS (480 Gs)

PYRUS (530 Gs or 600 Gs)

SUBTERRA (490 Gs)

VENTUS (520 Gs, 550 Gs, 570 Gs, or 600 Gs)

OTHER FORMS

BAKUBRONZE PYRUS (660 Gs)
BAKULYTE PYRUS (500 Gs)

FOR EVOLUTION CHAIN, FLIP TO PAGE 17.

SCRAPER

What's that scurrying across the battlefield? It's Scraper, a mechanical Bakugan. Scraper may be small but it can do plenty of damage with the two spikes on the end of its tail. It uses its horns and fangs to protect itself from damage. Scraper can combine with other Bakugan to form the Special Attack Bakugan Maxus Helios.

AVAILABLE ATTRIBUTES

- Aquos (540 Gs)
- Haos (580 Gs)
- Pyrus (550 Gs)
- Subterra (600 Gs or 660 Gs)
- Ventus (500 Gs, 590 Gs, or 700 Gs)

OTHER FORMS

BakuBronze Ventus (620 Gs, 690 Gs, or 730 Gs)
BakuMutation Aquos (530 Gs or 550 Gs)
BakuMutuation Haos (720 Gs or 760 Gs)
BakuMutuation Ventus (690 Gs or 730 Gs)

SHADOW VULCAN

Shadow Vulcan is one of the strongest Bakugan on New Vestroia, and it gains even more power when it battles on Earth. It towers over most opponents and assaults them with rocket punches that shoot out from its fists. Shadow Vulcan also has great defenses. The spinning rings on its body light up to deflect enemy fire, and it can catch and absorb fireballs in its fists.

SEEN WITH: VEXOS BRAWLER GUS GRAV.

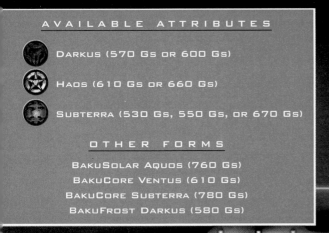

AVAILABLE ATTRIBUTES

- DARKUS (570 Gs OR 600 Gs)
- HAOS (610 Gs OR 660 Gs)
- SUBTERRA (530 Gs, 550 Gs, OR 670 Gs)

OTHER FORMS

BAKUSOLAR AQUOS (760 Gs)
BAKUCORE VENTUS (610 Gs)
BAKUCORE SUBTERRA (780 Gs)
BAKUFROST DARKUS (580 Gs)

EVOLUTION CHAIN

SHADOW VULCAN

⋙

PREMO VULCAN

SPINDLE

Spindle resembles a mechanical snake. Instead of scales, its body is covered with light and sturdy metallic fiber. And this snake has claws built for shredding any challenger. Any foe that escapes Spindle's claws has to deal with the blaster ray that emerges from its back to fire on multiple Bakugan at once. Spindle can combine with other Bakugan to form the Special Attack Bakugan Maxus Helios.

AVAILABLE ATTRIBUTES

- AQUOS (550 Gs or 640 Gs)
- HAOS (550 Gs)
- PYRUS (480 Gs, 620 Gs, or 710 Gs)
- VENTUS (530 Gs)

OTHER FORMS

BAKUBRONZE AQUOS (650 Gs)

STUG

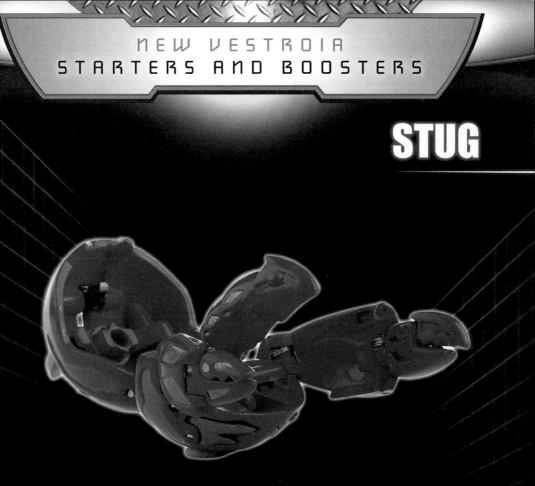

Have you ever seen a hermit crab scuttling around in the sand? Stug can maneuver like that on the field with its four legs to avoid attacks. But this is no child's pet. Stug's pincers have a sharp surprise inside: spikes! It also has spikes on its shell to protect it from damage.

SEEN WITH: MYLENE OF THE VEXOS. SHE RESURRECTED THIS EXTINCT BAKUGAN AS AN ENERGY BODY.

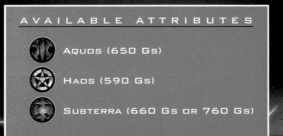

AVAILABLE ATTRIBUTES

AQUOS (650 Gs)

HAOS (590 Gs)

SUBTERRA (660 Gs OR 760 Gs)

THUNDER WILDA

When Wilda evolves, it becomes three times stronger. This massive Bakugan can harness Subterra energy to tap into the power of the earth under its feet. It shoots mega mud balls and tree vines from its mighty hands to take down its foes.

SEEN WITH: MIRA CLAY OF THE BAKUGAN RESISTANCE. HER SUBTERRA WILDA EVOLVED INTO THUNDER WILDA.

EVOLUTION CHAIN

WILDA

THUNDER WILDA

AVAILABLE ATTRIBUTES

 SUBTERRA (500 Gs, 630 Gs, AND 750 Gs)

VENTUS (710 Gs)

OTHER FORMS

BAKUBRONZE SUBTERRA (650 Gs)
BAKULYTE SUBTERRA (690 Gs)

ULTRA DRAGONOID

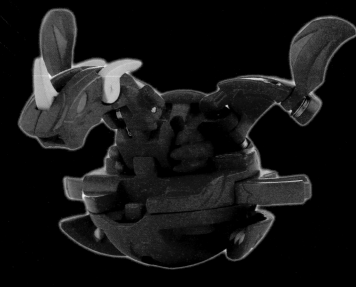

When Ultra Dragonoid evolves from Hyper Dragonoid, it gains greater speed after its wings double in size. Its attack also gets stronger thanks to multiple claws that tick out all over its body. Like all Dragonoid forms, Ultra Dragonoid shoots fireballs—but his are invisible, perfect for sneak attacks!.

SEEN WITH: DAN KUSO. ULTRA DRAGONOID IS ONE OF THE EVOLVED FORMS OF DAN'S GUARDIAN BAKUGAN, DRAGO.

AVAILABLE ATTRIBUTES

- AQUOS (540 Gs)
- HAOS (480 Gs or 580 Gs)
- PYRUS (470 Gs, 580 Gs, 650 Gs, or 700 Gs)
- SUBTERRA (450 Gs or 680 Gs)
- VENTUS (500 Gs or 650 Gs)

OTHER FORMS

DEKA PYRUS (660 Gs)
DUAL ATTRIBUTE BAKUGAN
PYRUS/HAOS (500 Gs)

FOR EVOLUTION CHAIN, FLIP TO PAGE 17.

VERIAS

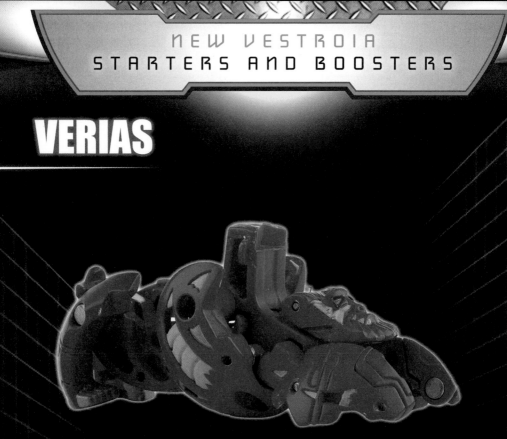

You'll know when this Bakugan is about to attack when it lets loose with a screeching battle cry. Then ape-like Verias will use its long staff to vault across the field, shooting a blinding beam of light from the purple jewel on its forehead. The staff also protects Verias from attacks, along with its thick fur. Verias is also a great climber, which helps it avoid enemies.

SEEN WITH: VEXOS
BRAWLER VOLT LUSTER,
WHO USES A HAOS
VERIAS.

AVAILABLE ATTRIBUTES

AQUOS (510 Gs, 630 Gs, OR 740 Gs)

HAOS (625 Gs)

VENTUS (650 Gs)

OTHER FORMS

BAKULYTE AQUOS (710 Gs)

VIPER HELIOS

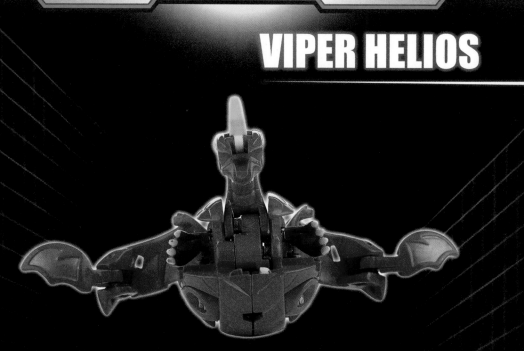

This vicious Bakugan grows crueler with each evolution. Its body is built for defense: Spikes cover its body, thick skin protects its legs, and its long tail lashes out to fend off foes. But Viper Helios doesn't have to worry about enemies getting too close—its fiery breath can melt metal!

SEEN WITH: VESTOS BRAWLER SPECTRA PHANTOM.

AVAILABLE ATTRIBUTES

AQUOS (490 Gs, 650 Gs, OR 730 Gs)

DARKUS (550 Gs OR 610 Gs)

HAOS (730 Gs OR 770 Gs)

PYRUS (720 Gs)

SUBTERRA (600 Gs)

VENTUS (660 Gs OR 770 Gs)

OTHER FORMS

BAKUEXOSKIN HAOS (740 Gs)

BAKUFROST AQUOS (550 Gs, 570 Gs, 750 Gs, OR 770 Gs)

BAKULYTE PYRUS (650 Gs)

BAKUSOLAR SUBTERRA (570 Gs)

BAKUSOLAR VENTUS (770 Gs), CLEAR (720 Gs)

DEKA SUBTERRA (620 Gs)

FOR EVOLUTION CHAIN, FLIP TO PAGE 77.

WILDA

Wilda rocks the field with her deafening battle cry. She's a massive monster made of hardened rock and clay. That slows her down, but it also allows her to take a lot of damage. Before attacking, Wilda shakes up opponents by pounding the ground with her giant fists. Then she finishes them off with a karate chop.

SEEN WITH:
MIRA CLAY OF
THE BAKUGAN
RESISTANCE,
WHO HAD A
SUBTERRA
WILDA THAT
EVOLVED INTO
THUNDER WILDA.

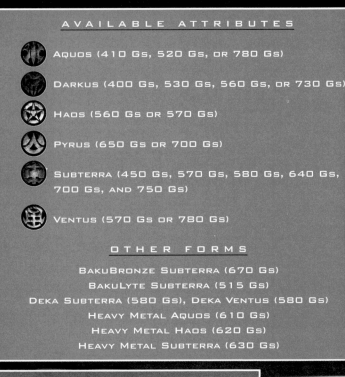

AVAILABLE ATTRIBUTES

AQUOS (410 Gs, 520 Gs, or 780 Gs)

DARKUS (400 Gs, 530 Gs, 560 Gs, or 730 Gs)

HAOS (560 Gs or 570 Gs)

PYRUS (650 Gs or 700 Gs)

SUBTERRA (450 Gs, 570 Gs, 580 Gs, 640 Gs, 700 Gs, and 750 Gs)

VENTUS (570 Gs or 780 Gs)

OTHER FORMS

BAKUBRONZE SUBTERRA (670 Gs)
BAKULYTE SUBTERRA (515 Gs)
DEKA SUBTERRA (580 Gs), DEKA VENTUS (580 Gs)
HEAVY METAL AQUOS (610 Gs)
HEAVY METAL HAOS (620 Gs)
HEAVY METAL SUBTERRA (630 Gs)

FOR EVOLUTION CHAIN, FLIP TO PAGE 98.

fast, Wired whizzes across the battlefield, avoiding attacks. This
al Bakugan might not be big and brawny, but it's more than ca
amage. It pecks at foes with its indestructible beak, and shreds
razor-tipped feathers and wickedly sharp claws.

H: VEXOS BRAWLER LYNC VOLAN.

AVAILABLE ATTRIBUTES

AQUOS (630 Gs)

HAOS (500 Gs, 620 Gs, OR 710 Gs)

PYRUS (600 Gs)

SUBTERRA (520 Gs)

OTHER FORMS

BAKUMUTATION HAOS (570 Gs OR 620 Gs)
BAKUMUTATION SUBTERRA (740 Gs OR 770 Gs)

ALPHA HYDRANOID

This evolved form of Hydranoid comes equipped with metal armor that can take blow after blow. He can launch fireballs from each of his mouths that are capable of melting just about anything. Alpha Hydranoid prefers fighting at night so he can blend into the darkness and catch enemies by surprise.

SEEN WITH: MASQUERADE.

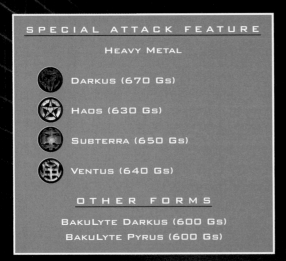

SPECIAL ATTACK FEATURE

HEAVY METAL

DARKUS (670 Gs)

HAOS (630 Gs)

SUBTERRA (650 Gs)

VENTUS (640 Gs)

OTHER FORMS

BAKULYTE DARKUS (600 Gs)
BAKULYTE PYRUS (600 Gs)

FOR EVOLUTION CHAIN, FLIP TO PAGE 18.

ALPHA PERCIVAL CYCLONE

Alpha Percival Cyclone combines strength, accuracy, and efficiency to make it one of the most useful Bakugan to have in your arsenal. If those qualities weren't enough, this Bakugan gets a boost of Cyclone power. It can spin hard and fast enough to take down some of the biggest opponents on the field!

SPECIAL ATTACK FEATURE

SPIN TOP

- DARKUS (700 Gs)
- HAOS (710 Gs)
- SUBTERRA (700 Gs)

FOR EVOLUTION CHAIN, FLIP TO PAGE 66.

BOOST INGRAM

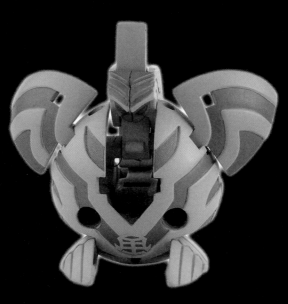

Boost Ingram can fly super fast with its special wings, but it pays a price: lost energy. The thorns on its head protect it. If Boost Ingram is under attack, it releases a loud cry to call on its friends for help.

SPECIAL ATTACK FEATURE

JUMPING

- DARKUS (680 Gs)
- SUBTERRA (650 Gs)
- VENTUS (670 Gs)

FOR EVOLUTION CHAIN, FLIP TO PAGE 71.

DELTA DRAGONOID II

When Dragonoid evolves into Delta Dragonoid, he gets an extra set of wings and a pointy pitchfork on the end of his tail. This dangerous dragon-like creature's body is covered with armor to protect him from attacks..

SEEN WITH: DAN KUSO. DELTA DRAGONOID FIRST APPEARED AFTER DRAG-ONOID EVOLVED DURING A THREE-WAY BATTLE BETWEEN DAN, RUNO, AND MARUCHO AGAINST JULIO, KLAUS, AND CHAN LEE.

SPECIAL ATTACK FEATURES

HEAVY METAL

- DARKUS (550 Gs)
- SUBTERRA (600 Gs)
- VENTUS (520 Gs OR 580 Gs)

REVERSE ELEMENT

- AQUOS (550 Gs)
- HAOS (530 Gs)
- PYRUS (560 Gs)

DUAL ELFIN REVOLUTION

SPECIAL ATTACK FEATURE

DOUBLE ROULETTE (ONE EACH OF THE THREE
G-POWERS AND ATTRIBUTE CHANGES LISTED IS
RANDOMLY GENERATED ON EACH ROLL)

AQUOS	760 – 640 – 550 Gs	HAOS – PYRUS – SUBTERRA
DARKUS	750 – 650 – 550 Gs	HAOS – VENTUS – AQUOS
HAOS	750 – 650 – 560 Gs	DARKUS – AQUOS – SUBTERRA
VENTUS	750 – 660 – 610 Gs	SUBTERRA – DARKUS – AQUOS

This Bakugan darts back and forth across the field, avoiding enemy fire. Even though she looks like something from a fairy tale, Dual Elfin Revolution is intimidating to her enemies. Not many Bakugan are eager to face an opponent that can gain new abilities and strengths instantly in the heat of battle!

SEEN WITH: PREYAS, HER GOOD FRIEND.

FOR EVOLUTION CHAIN, FLIP TO PAGE 72.

ELFIN

Elfin has a sense of humor and a lot of energy in battle—just like her good friend, Preyas. Elfin's attribute-changing power gives her an advantage over almost any opponent. She can also shoot arrows from her frog-like fingers.

SEEN WITH: MARUCHO. WHEN HE WENT TO NEW VESTROIA TO FIND PREYAS, ELFIN AGREED TO BECOME HIS BAKUGAN AND BATTLE WITH HIM AGAINST THE VEXOS.

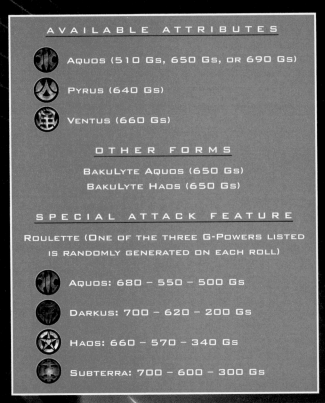

AVAILABLE ATTRIBUTES

Aquos (510 Gs, 650 Gs, or 690 Gs)

Pyrus (640 Gs)

Ventus (660 Gs)

OTHER FORMS

BakuLyte Aquos (650 Gs)
BakuLyte Haos (650 Gs)

SPECIAL ATTACK FEATURE

Roulette (One of the three G-Powers listed is randomly generated on each roll)

Aquos: 680 – 550 – 500 Gs

Darkus: 700 – 620 – 200 Gs

Haos: 660 – 570 – 340 Gs

Subterra: 700 – 600 – 300 Gs

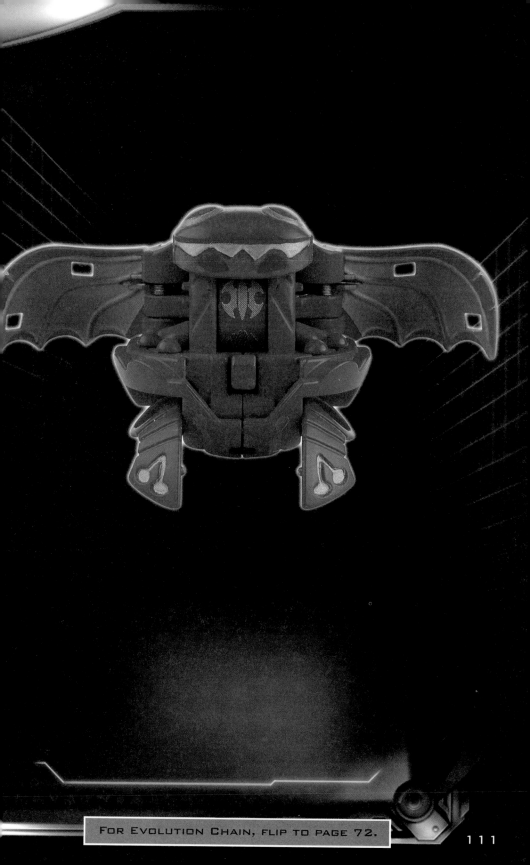

FOR EVOLUTION CHAIN, FLIP TO PAGE 72.

ELICO

Elico looks like a soldier or knight with spiked armor and helmet on his head. This brute is loaded with features to use during an attack. The six tentacles that grow from his back can wrap around a foe, rendering them defenseless. Six sharp blades extend from his arms. Elico specializes in water battles. He can breathe underwater, and shoots a powerful blast from a golden diamond on his body.

SEEN WITH: VEXOS BRAWLER MYLENE PHARAOH.

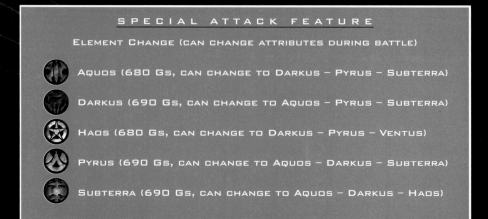

SPECIAL ATTACK FEATURE

ELEMENT CHANGE (CAN CHANGE ATTRIBUTES DURING BATTLE)

AQUOS (680 GS, CAN CHANGE TO DARKUS – PYRUS – SUBTERRA)

DARKUS (690 GS, CAN CHANGE TO AQUOS – PYRUS – SUBTERRA)

HAOS (680 GS, CAN CHANGE TO DARKUS – PYRUS – VENTUS)

PYRUS (690 GS, CAN CHANGE TO AQUOS – DARKUS – SUBTERRA)

SUBTERRA (690 GS, CAN CHANGE TO AQUOS – DARKUS – HAOS)

HYPER CYCLONE DRAGONOID

This Bakugan has the twisting power of a terrifying tornado to tear down its enemies. To avoid enemy fire, it can escape with super speed. The spikes all over its body also add to its defense.

SPECIAL ATTACK FEATURE

SPIN TOP

AQUOS (650 Gs)

PYRUS (700 Gs)

SUBTERRA (690 Gs)

FOR EVOLUTION CHAIN, FLIP TO PAGE 17.

INFINITY DRAGONOID

The Infinity Core is one of the power sources of Vestroia. Wavern held it to protect it from her power-hungry brother, Naga. When she could no longer control it, she transferred it to Dan's Drago.

When Drago absorbed the Infinity Core, he evolved into an Infinity Dragonoid. He gained the power to see through walls, and attacked enemies using his three powerful tails. This is one of the most powerful forms Drago has ever taken.

SPECIAL ATTACK FEATURE

HEAVY METAL

AQUOS (650 Gs)

DARKUS (660 Gs)

PYRUS (680 Gs)

OTHER FORMS

BAKULYTE DARKUS (640 Gs)
BAKULYTE PYRUS (650 Gs)
BAKULYTE SUBTERRA (660 Gs)

FOR EVOLUTION CHAIN, FLIP TO PAGE 17

MOONLIGHT MONARUS

This monster may look like a butterfly, but it doesn't flutter away in the face of danger. Moonlight Monarus uses its huge wings to make itself look larger and more dangerous to its enemies.
It can also use its wings to quickly dodge an attack. This Special Attack Bakugan has an extra advantage because it can battle in the dark. Its wings will light up to blind its opponents.

SPECIAL ATTACK FEATURE

ELECTRONIC (LIGHTS UP)

HAOS (710 Gs)

PYRUS (720 Gs)

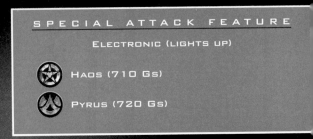

FOR EVOLUTION CHAIN, FLIP TO PAGE 38.

NEO VORTEX DRAGONOID

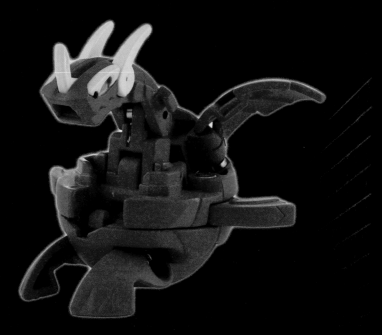

When this Dragonoid lands on a Gate card, he can create whirling fire tornadoes to blow his opponents off the field. Besides this Special Attack power, Neo Vortex Dragonoid has multiple wings and can camouflage by changing his body color. Bright diamonds on his body blind his foes with their brilliance.

SPECIAL ATTACK FEATURE

SPIN TOP

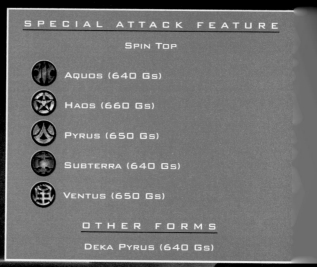

- AQUOS (640 Gs)
- HAOS (660 Gs)
- PYRUS (650 Gs)
- SUBTERRA (640 Gs)
- VENTUS (650 Gs)

OTHER FORMS

DEKA PYRUS (640 Gs)

FOR EVOLUTION CHAIN, FLIP TO PAGE 17.

ORBIT HELIOS

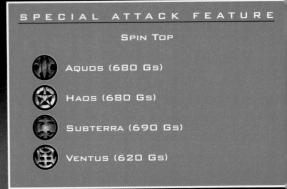

This dragon-like Bakugan is strong, compact, and powerful. Its body is covered with sharp horns for both attack power and defense. Razor-like claws on its wings slash away at foes. When Orbit Helios spins, its strong tail can knock down just about anything in its path.

SPECIAL ATTACK FEATURE

SPIN TOP

- AQUOS (680 Gs)
- HAOS (680 Gs)
- SUBTERRA (690 Gs)
- VENTUS (620 Gs)

FOR EVOLUTION CHAIN, FLIP TO PAGE 77.

PERCIVAL VORTEX

n this form, loyal Bakugan Percival gains many awesome attack and defense features. Four horns on its shoulders and a strong gold shield protect it from harm. It olds two gleaming double-edged swords to slice away at foes. When this Special Attack akugan spins, it moves so st that the light around bends. This warps the sion of its opponent, ving Percival Vortex the lvantage in battle.

EEN WITH: ACE
F THE BAKUGAN
ESISTANCE.

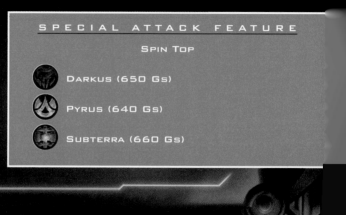

SPECIAL ATTACK FEATURE

SPIN TOP

- DARKUS (650 Gs)
- PYRUS (640 Gs)
- SUBTERRA (660 Gs)

FOR EVOLUTION CHAIN, FLIP TO PAGE 66.

PREMO VULCAN

This Bakugan stands tall on the field—taller than most of his opponents. Premo Vulcan's power is concentrated in his mighty fists. In a close-range fight, his super-strong punches can shatter the strongest armor. If his target is far away, Primo Vulcan can fire his detachable fists like cannonballs at his foes.

SEEN WITH: VEXOS BRAWLER GUS GRAV.

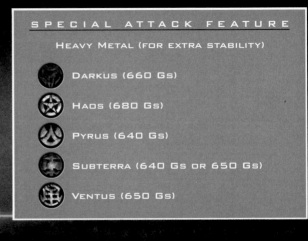

SPECIAL ATTACK FEATURE
HEAVY METAL (FOR EXTRA STABILITY)
DARKUS (660 Gs)
HAOS (680 Gs)
PYRUS (640 Gs)
SUBTERRA (640 Gs or 650 Gs)
VENTUS (650 Gs)

FOR EVOLUTION CHAIN, FLIP TO PAGE 95.

SPIN DRAGONOID

When this Dragonoid gets moving, it creates a tornado-like funnel that can do as much devastating damage as a savage storm. Spin Dragonoid can strengthen its attack by shooting sharp horns from its forehead. And while this Bakugan is big and strong, it can glide across the air on the gentlest of breezes.

SPECIAL ATTACK FEATURE

SPIN TOP

- HAOS (650 Gs)
- PYRUS (670 Gs)

FOR EVOLUTION CHAIN, FLIP TO PAGE 17.

SPIN RAVENOID

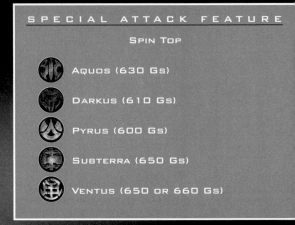

When this Bakugan spins, it digs into the ground like a powerful drill. Then it can startle its opponent with an underground attack using its unbreakable claws. Its massive wings provide an excellent defensive shield.

SPECIAL ATTACK FEATURE

SPIN TOP

- AQUOS (630 Gs)
- DARKUS (610 Gs)
- PYRUS (600 Gs)
- SUBTERRA (650 Gs)
- VENTUS (650 OR 660 Gs)

FOR EVOLUTION CHAIN, FLIP TO PAGE 42.

TURBINE DRAGONOID

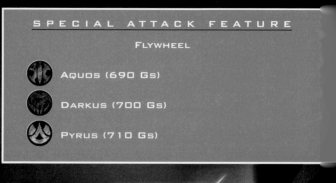

This Bakugan is equipped with power equal to the turbine engines of a jet airplane. This extra power allows Turbine Dragonoid to explode with one of the most scorching fireballs a Bakugan can create. This towering terror can strike out with its mighty horn, knocking down a foe in one blow. Its metal-covered wings can wrap around Turbine Dragonoid's body like a shield.

SPECIAL ATTACK FEATURE

FLYWHEEL

- AQUOS (690 Gs)
- DARKUS (700 Gs)
- PYRUS (710 Gs)

FOR EVOLUTION CHAIN, FLIP TO PAGE 17.

1

TURBINE HADES

When this Turbine Bakugan spins, it can create powerful winds to send its foes flying off of the field. Turbine Hades has two extra, smaller heads that can detach and shoot at an enemy like missiles. And if an opponent is able to get close enough to attack, this Bakugan can slash at it with its sharp claws.

AVAILABLE ATTRIBUTES

Aquos (570 Gs)

Darkus (710 Gs)

Ventus (650 Gs)

OTHER FORMS

BakuBronze Darkus (630 Gs)
BakuLyte Aquos (550 Gs)

SPECIAL ATTACK FEATURE

Flywheel

Darkus (640 Gs)

Haos (650 Gs)

Pyrus (650 Gs)

Subterra (640 Gs)

FOR EVOLUTION CHAIN, FLIP TO PAGE 76.

TURBINE HELIOS

Turbine Helios combines the ultimate power of fire and wings in its attack. It spins to create hurricane-force gales while shooting multiple fireballs at its opponents. For defense, this Bakugan uses the two green spots on its wings to deflect enemy blasts.

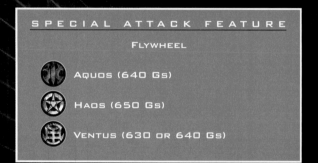

SPECIAL ATTACK FEATURE

FLYWHEEL

AQUOS (640 Gs)

HAOS (650 Gs)

VENTUS (630 OR 640 Gs)

For Evolution Chain, flip to page 77.

ULTRA DRAGONOID TYPHOON

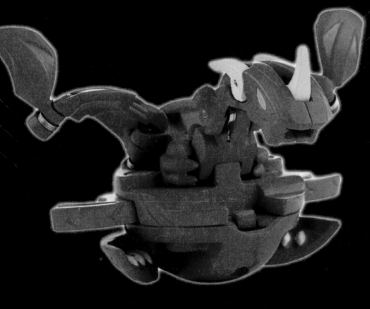

Multiple wings allow this form of Ultra Dragonoid to create powerful winds while flying with amazing speed and accuracy. It targets foes with a barrage of blazing fireballs.

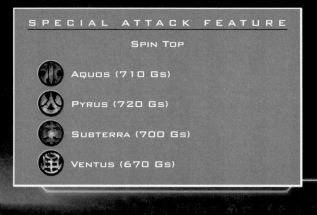

SPECIAL ATTACK FEATURE

SPIN TOP

AQUOS (710 Gs)

PYRUS (720 Gs)

SUBTERRA (700 Gs)

VENTUS (670 Gs)

FOR EVOLUTION CHAIN, FLIP TO PAGE 17.

VANDARUS

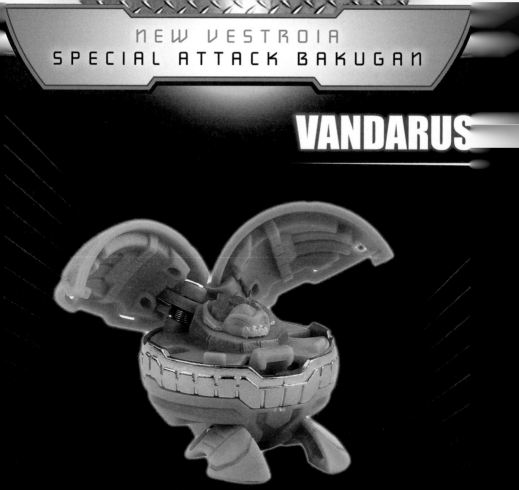

This mammoth monster is a big brute with huge fists that he uses to smash its opponents. He's a frightening sight on the field, with flaming hair and green, glowing eyes that can see through walls. The armored belt he wears protects him from damage during battle.

SPECIAL ATTACK FEATURE
HEAVY METAL

- AQUOS (660 Gs)
- DARKUS (610 Gs)
- PYRUS (620 Gs)
- SUBTERRA (640 Gs)

THE BAKUGAN TRAP

Having a Bakugan Trap in your arsenal can be just what you need to turn the tide in a difficult battle. You can surprise your opponents by combining it with one or more other Bakugan to create a new monster with an extra boost of power.

BALITON

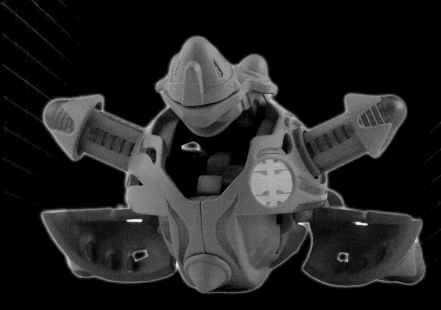

AVAILABLE ATTRIBUTES

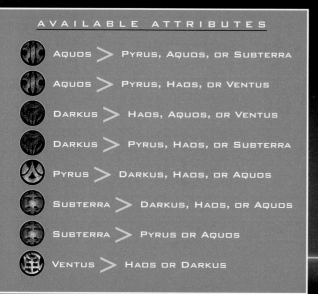

AQUOS > PYRUS, AQUOS, OR SUBTERRA

AQUOS > PYRUS, HAOS, OR VENTUS

DARKUS > HAOS, AQUOS, OR VENTUS

DARKUS > PYRUS, HAOS, OR SUBTERRA

PYRUS > DARKUS, HAOS, OR AQUOS

SUBTERRA > DARKUS, HAOS, OR AQUOS

SUBTERRA > PYRUS OR AQUOS

VENTUS > HAOS OR DARKUS

The first thing you'll notice about this sturdy Bakugan are the horns sticking out all over its body, including its tail. Baliton can swing this spiky tail like a baseball bat to pound its foes. Like Wilda, Baliton is slow and heavy, but it uses its weight as an advantage to crush the opposition.

BRACHIUM

Brachium looks like a snake—but not like any snake you've ever seen before. First of all, its body is covered with metal. It has one head on each end of its body, and each head is equipped with a blaster that zaps energy from other Bakugan. Brachium can lash out with its long body like a whip, or wrap around a foe to render it defenseless.

AVAILABLE ATTRIBUTES

HAOS > DARKUS

CARLSNAUT

AVAILABLE ATTRIBUTES

AQUOS > PYRUS

HAOS > DARKUS

PYRUS > AQUOS

VENTUS > SUBTERRA

Opponents quiver in fear when Carlsnaut lunges toward them with its sharp blades twirling. This Bakugan can also attack with power-packed water balls that can knock foes down like bowling pins.

HOUND

...hunting dog, Dark Hound can move with amazing speed c... ...o are hiding. But Dark Hound can do a trick an ordinary d... ...ility to change a Bakugan's attribute.

AVAILABLE ATTRIBUTES

DARKUS > HAOS

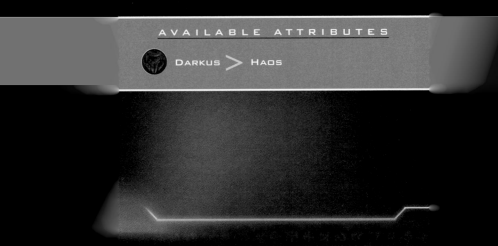

DYN

...ks like a big mechanical bug with six fast-moving legs and s...
...akugan's most amazing feature is its three red, glowing eyes...
...namo's eyes will become hypnotized and helpless to fight ba...

AVAILABLE ATTRIBUTES

AQUOS > VENTUS, SUBTERRA, OR DARKUS

DARKUS > PYRUS, AQUOS, OR VENTUS

HAOS > VENTUS, AQUOS, OR PYRUS

SUBTERRA > DARKUS, HAOS, OR AQUOS

VENTUS > HAOS, DARKUS, OR PYRUS

PARTNERS WITH

BRONTES

FALCON FLY

Falcon Fly was designed for optimum performance on the field. Its dark color makes it hard to see at night. Its wings flap so fast that this Bakugan moves faster than a dragonfly. And its body is so thin that it's almost impossible to see when it's flying right at you. Once it gets close, Falcon Fly will shoot laser beams from its eyes!

AVAILABLE ATTRIBUTES

AQUOS > SUBTERRA OR VENTUS

HAOS > PYRUS OR AQUOS

VENTUS > HAOS OR DARKUS

PARTNERS WITH

PERCIVAL

FIRE SCORPION

Watch out for Fire Scorpion's claws—if they clamp down on you, this Bakugan will give you a thrashing you'll never forget. Foes who attack Fire Scorpion have trouble penetrating its hard armor. But this tough armor is light, which allows this Bakugan to move quickly around the field.

AVAILABLE ATTRIBUTES

PYRUS > SUBTERRA OR AQUOS

SUBTERRA > VENTUS OR AQUOS

FORTRESS

This Bakugan Trap starts out as a cube, then unfolds to become a soldier bearing ten cannons. Rockets on the bottom of Fortress's feet allow it to quickly avoid enemy fire.

AVAILABLE ATTRIBUTES

AQUOS > DARKUS OR VENTUS

DARKUS > SUBTERRA OR AQUOS

PYRUS > DARKUS OR HAOS

SUBTERRA > HAOS OR PYRUS

VENTUS > PYRUS RO HAOS

PARTNERS WITH

HADES

GRAFIAS

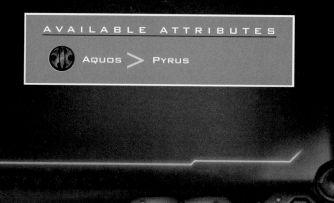

The main feature of this Bakugan is a wrench-like clamp that it can use to grab opponents. Most Bakugan have a hard time getting away from the grasp of Grafias. This Bakugan also has excellent hearing, so it can track foes over long distances.

AVAILABLE ATTRIBUTES

AQUOS > PYRUS

GRAKAS HOUND

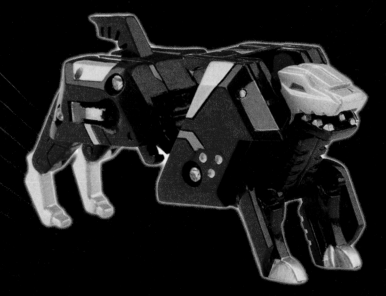

If you hear Grakas Hound growl, it means he's about to attack. This mechanical canine doesn't chomp on doggy treats—he prefers to tear apart metal with its powerful jaws and teeth.

AVAILABLE ATTRIBUTES

SUBTERRA > VENTUS

HEXAD

serpent-like Bakugan Trap is loaded for battle. It can strike from either of its body using one of its two heads. Its camouflaged outer body all eak up on enemies, and it can see in all directions with the three eyes ead. Hexados shoots out arrows from the blue holes located all over it. When Hexados is attacked, a shield protects its core, and sharp horns k ds safe.

AVAILABLE ATTRIBUTES

HAOS > DARKUS, PYRUS, SUBTERRA, OR AQUOS

PYRUS > AQUOS, SUBTERRA, DARKUS, OR VENTUS

SUBTERRA > VENTUS, PYRUS, DARKUS, OR HAOS

PARTNERS WITH

VIPER HELIOS

HEXSTAR

Hexstar is one of the strongest Bakugan around. This powerhouse stomps around on four legs and threatens enemies by thrashing its horny tail. Spikes on its back protect Hexstar from attack.

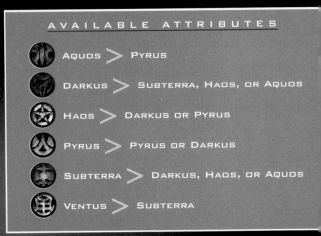

AVAILABLE ATTRIBUTES

AQUOS > PYRUS

DARKUS > SUBTERRA, HAOS, OR AQUOS

HAOS > DARKUS OR PYRUS

PYRUS > PYRUS OR DARKUS

SUBTERRA > DARKUS, HAOS, OR AQUOS

VENTUS > SUBTERRA

HYLASH

Zap! Hylash can shoot a laser beam from its forehead to stun opponents. For a close-up attack, it will run circles around foes and then smash them with its sharp spikes. The huge shields on Hylash's shoulders can withstand heavy blows.

AVAILABLE ATTRIBUTES

AQUOS > DARKUS, HAOS, OR VENTUS

DARKUS > SUBTERRA, PYRUS, OR VENTUS

HAOS > AQUOS OR VENTUS

PYRUS > DARKUS OR VENTUS

PARTNERS WITH

INGRAM

LEGIONOID

A snake with one head is scary enough—but this snake-like Bakugan opens up to reveal six heads! Each head can spit out a poison associated with one of the attributes.

AVAILABLE ATTRIBUTES

AQUOS > DARKUS, SUBTERRA, OR VENTUS

DARKUS > AQUOS, SUBTERRA, OR VENTUS

DARKUS > PYRUS, AQUOS, AND SUBTERRA

HAOS > PYRUS, SUBTERRA, AND AQUOS

PYRUS > SUBTERRA, VENTUS, AND DARKUS

SUBTERRA > PYRUS, AQUOS, AND DARKUS

VENTUS > AQUOS, SUBTERRA, OR DARKUS

VENTUS > HAOS, PYRUS, AND AQUOS

METALFENCER

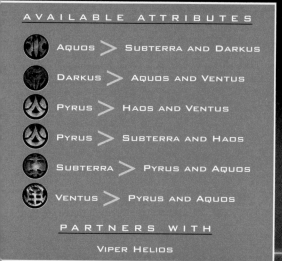

AVAILABLE ATTRIBUTES

AQUOS > SUBTERRA AND DARKUS

DARKUS > AQUOS AND VENTUS

PYRUS > HAOS AND VENTUS

PYRUS > SUBTERRA AND HAOS

SUBTERRA > PYRUS AND AQUOS

VENTUS > PYRUS AND AQUOS

PARTNERS WITH

VIPER HELIOS

Metalfencer can battle under almost any condition. If it's backed into a corner, it can freeze its opponents with its three eyes and then zap them with its sharp stinger. If it needs to attack from a safe distance, it can shoot lasers from its tail. Metalfencer can maneuver over almost any terrain with its four legs.

PIERCIAN

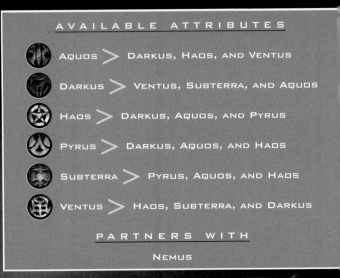

Want to try to knock down Piercian? Good luck. Its massive legs are like cement blocks, making it hard to take down this Bakugan. The enormous shields on its shoulders do double duty: They protect Piercian from harm, but can also detach to be used as weapons.

AVAILABLE ATTRIBUTES

AQUOS > DARKUS, HAOS, AND VENTUS

DARKUS > VENTUS, SUBTERRA, AND AQUOS

HAOS > DARKUS, AQUOS, AND PYRUS

PYRUS > DARKUS, AQUOS, AND HAOS

SUBTERRA > PYRUS, AQUOS, AND HAOS

VENTUS > HAOS, SUBTERRA, AND DARKUS

PARTNERS WITH

NEMUS

PYTHANTUS

This Bakugan burrows underground, boring through the dirt, and then . . . bam! It sneaks up on its foe, biting it with its sharp, poisonous fangs. The horns running along its body give Pythantus some extra protection.

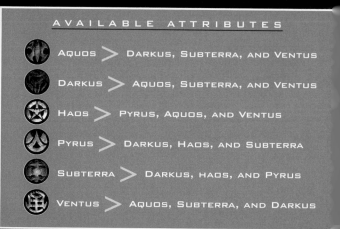

AVAILABLE ATTRIBUTES

AQUOS > DARKUS, SUBTERRA, AND VENTUS

DARKUS > AQUOS, SUBTERRA, AND VENTUS

HAOS > PYRUS, AQUOS, AND VENTUS

PYRUS > DARKUS, HAOS, AND SUBTERRA

SUBTERRA > DARKUS, HAOS, AND PYRUS

VENTUS > AQUOS, SUBTERRA, AND DARKUS

SCORPION

You won't find this Scorpion hiding under your bed. This giant towers over the battlefield on its six long legs. Scorpion snaps at foes with its strong pincers and whips them with its long, sharp tail. This Bakugan is protected by an exoskeleton that acts as a full-body shield.

AVAILABLE ATTRIBUTES

AQUOS > DARKUS OR HAOS

AQUOS > VENTUS OR SUBTERRA

DARKUS > PYRUS OR AQUOS

DARKUS > SUBTERRA OR VENTUS

HAOS > PYRUS OR AQUOS

PYRUS > DARKUS OR HAOS

PYRUS > VENTUS OR SUBTERRA

SUBTERRA > PYRUS OR AQUOS

VENTUS > DARKUS OR HAOS

VENTUS > PYRUS OR AQUOS

PARTNERS WITH

DRAGO

SPITARM

Spitarm soars through the sky, searching for enemies below. When it spots a foe, it swoops down and strikes with its poison-tipped stinger.

AVAILABLE ATTRIBUTES

VENTUS > SUBTERRA

SPYDERFENCER

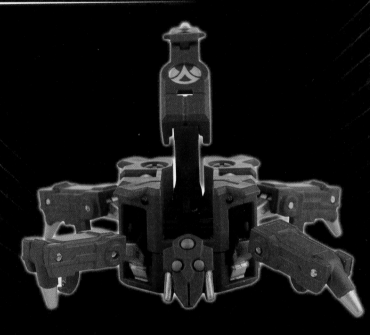

This spider-like Bakugan may be small in size, but that gives it an advantage. It can hide in tight spots and then spring out to surprise an enemy.

AVAILABLE ATTRIBUTES

PYRUS > AQUOS

TRIAD EL CON

Bakugan Trap opens up, he resembles an Aztec totem pole. V
an ancient statue, he fries foes with laser beam blasts. Triad
he's sturdy and can take a lot of punishment. He can also fly
e needs an air advantage.

AVAILABLE ATTRIBUTES

DARKUS > VENTUS, SUBTERRA, OR PYRUS

HAOS > VENTUS, SUBTERRA, OR PYRUS

PYRUS > DARKUS, HAOS, OR VENTUS

SUBTERRA > VENTUS, PYRUS, OR AQUOS

VENTUS > DARKUS, HAOS, OR PYRUS

TRIAD SPHINX

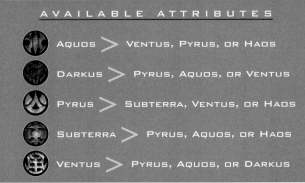

This Bakugan looks like something you might find in ancient Egypt. His mysterious green eyes can shoot out dangerous beams. His large headband protects his head from damage.

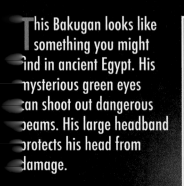

AVAILABLE ATTRIBUTES

AQUOS > VENTUS, PYRUS, OR HAOS

DARKUS > PYRUS, AQUOS, OR VENTUS

PYRUS > SUBTERRA, VENTUS, OR HAOS

SUBTERRA > PYRUS, AQUOS, OR HAOS

VENTUS > PYRUS, AQUOS, OR DARKUS

TRIPOD EPSILON

You're walking through the swamps of Vestroia when you think you see two red eyes staring at you from the leaves. It could be Tripod Epsilon, who can blend into his surroundings like a chameleon. Those red eyes can control the actions of his opponents. If you get too close, he might take a giant leap—he can travel great distances in just one round.

AVAILABLE ATTRIBUTES

AQUOS	>	SUBTERRA, DARKUS, OR PYRUS
DARKUS	>	HAOS, PYRUS, OR SUBTERRA
DARKUS	>	SUBTERRA, AQUOS, OR PYRUS
HAOS	>	AQUOS, DARKUS, OR PYRUS
PYRUS	>	AQUOS, DARKUS, OR VENTUS
SUBTERRA	>	AQUOS, DARKUS, OR PYRUS
VENTUS	>	HAOS, AQUOS, OR PYRUS

PARTNERS WITH

ELFIN

OD THETA

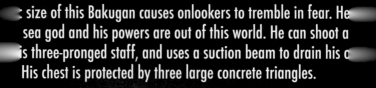

: size of this Bakugan causes onlookers to tremble in fear. He
sea god and his powers are out of this world. He can shoot a
is three-pronged staff, and uses a suction beam to drain his o
His chest is protected by three large concrete triangles.

: MYLENE OF THE VEXOS, WHO RESURRECTED IT F
JRM.

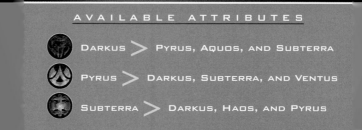

AVAILABLE ATTRIBUTES

DARKUS > PYRUS, AQUOS, AND SUBTERRA

PYRUS > DARKUS, SUBTERRA, AND VENTUS

SUBTERRA > DARKUS, HAOS, AND PYRUS

ZOACK

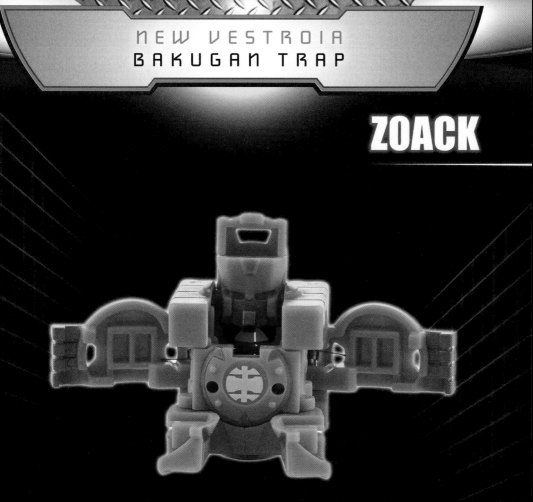

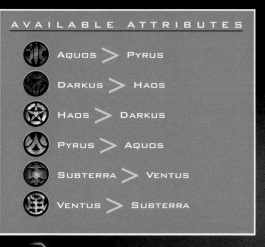

AVAILABLE ATTRIBUTES

- AQUOS > PYRUS
- DARKUS > HAOS
- HAOS > DARKUS
- PYRUS > AQUOS
- SUBTERRA > VENTUS
- VENTUS > SUBTERRA

If Zoack wants to give you a hug, you might want to politely say no. This massive stone monster crushes foes in its powerful arms. And Zoack can take as much as it dishes out. It's difficult to damage this tough guy.

157

MAXUS BAKUGAN

When you need maximum power during battle, it's time to use your Maxus Bakugan! It takes seven different Bakugan to make each Maxus Bakugan. Each Bakugan or Bakugan Trap brings a new skill or strength to the party, making Maxus Bakugan some of the most impressive monsters you'll ever see in a brawl.

MAXUS DRAGONOID

Seven Bakugan combine to form this Dragonoid that has the power to devastate its enemies. This super seven includes Grakas Hound, Dark Hound, Grafias, Brachium, Spitarm, Spyderfencer, and Neo Dragonoid. These Bakugan can also be used individually in battle.

SEEN WITH: DAN, WHEN DAN'S DRAGO WAS BATTLING MAXUS HELIOS. DRAGO HAD TO TRANSFORM INTO A MECHANICAL BAKUGAN TO TAKE ON THIS ROBOTIC BEAST.

MAXUS DRAGO INCLUDES:

BRACHIUM
PAGE 134

GRAFIAS
PAGE 141

SPITARM
PAGE 151

DARK HOUND
PAGE 136

GRAKAS HOUND
PAGE 142

SPYDERFENCER
PAGE 152

NEO DRAGONOID
PAGE 90

FOR EVOLUTION CHAIN, FLIP TO PAGE 17.

MAXUS HELIOS

MAXUS HELIOS INCLUDES:

FENCER
PAGE 73

HELIOS
PAGE 77

SCRAPER
PAGE 94

FOXBAT
PAGE 74

KLAWGOR
PAGE 81

SPINDLE
PAGE 96

LEEFRAM
PAGE 82

This towering terror dominates the battlefield! Seven Bakugan join together to form it: Helios, Scraper, Klawgor, Foxbat, Fencer, Leefram, and Spindle. Separately, each one is a force to be reckoned with.

FOR EVOLUTION CHAIN, FLIP TO PAGE 77.

NEW BATTLES, NEW BAKUGAN, AND A NEW ADVENTURE

Dan and Drago have saved Earth before—but now our planet is in danger again. The Gundalian Protectors of the Dark Bakugan and the Twelve Orders have attacked Neathia, a peaceful planet, and now they've set their sights on Earth. They invade Earth by entering through virtual reality Bakugan Interspace.

In their fight against the Gundalian Invaders, Dan encounters new enemies and new Bakugan with abilities he's never seen before. The brawlers will also use new Bakugan Battle Gear to add attack and defensive powers to their Bakugan. Read on to find out more about what's waiting in

AKWIMOS

If you're battling underwater, you need Akwimos on your team. This Bakugan can create devastating attacks using water energy balls. Besides having a great sense of humor, Akwimos has a special talent on the field. If he tucks his claws under both hands, he can break and cancel out the powers of the Gate card.

SEEN WITH: MARUCHO.

AVAILABLE ATTRIBUTES

AQUOS (670 Gs, 800 Gs, or 810 Gs)

PYRUS (640 Gs or 660 Gs)

SUBTERRA (650 Gs or 790 Gs)

OTHER FORMS

BAKULYTE DARKUS (600 Gs)
BAKULYTE PYRUS (600 Gs)
CLEAR (660 Gs or 800 Gs)
STEALTH DARKUS (790 Gs)

ARANAUT

What's that shining in the sky? A rocket? No, it's Aranaut, with sparkles like platinum.

Some Bakugan are strong in one area, like attacks, but weak in ot like speed. Not Aranaut. His skills are evenly balanced between at defense skills, speed, and reflexes. That makes him a good match any kind of opponent.

When Aranaut does attack, he emits an electromagnetic field from o paralyze foes.

SEEN WITH: BRAWLER FABIA.

AVAILABLE ATTRIBUTES

- Aquos (650 Gs or 770 Gs)
- Darkus (760 Gs)
- Haos (680 Gs, 740 Gs, 760 Gs, or 800 Gs)
- Pyrus (750 Gs)
- Ventus (620 Gs)

OTHER FORMS

Stealth Night Darkus (810 Gs)

AVIOR

This loyal Bakugan can be dangerous in the heat of battle. He throws out flames hot enough to melt rocks! Avior can also blast opponents with impact waves he shoots from his mouth.

SEEN WITH: REN'S TEAM.

AVAILABLE ATTRIBUTES

VENTUS (740 Gs)

OTHER FORMS

BAKUDOUBLESTIKE HAOS (760 Gs – DS POWER 90)
BAKUDOUBLESTRIKE PYRUS (660 Gs – DS POWER 90)
BAKUDOUBLESTRIKE VENTUS (690 Gs – DS POWER 60, 870 Gs – DS POWER 30)
BAKUEXOSKIN AQUOS (740 Gs)
BAKUEXOSKIN DARKUS (620 Gs OR 700 Gs)
BAKUEXOSKIN HAOS (600 Gs OR 740 Gs)
BAKUEXOSKIN PYRUS (630 Gs OR 740 Gs)
BAKUEXOSKIN SUBTERRA (630 Gs OR 750 Gs)
BAKUEXOSKIN VENTUS (600 Gs)
DEKA SILVER (760 Gs)
DESERT ROCK STEALTH SUBTERRA (800 Gs)

CONTESTIR

Off the field, Contestir is calm and dignified. He's wise and doesn't get angry easily. But when he gets on the field, watch out! This Bakugan attacks quickly, unleashing glowing energy waves to blast his opponents.

SEEN WITH: REN'S TEAM.

AVAILABLE ATTRIBUTES

DARKUS (630 Gs)

HAOS (800 Gs)

SUBTERRA (860 Gs)

VENTUS (670 Gs)

OTHER FORMS

BAKULYTE HAOS (800 Gs)
BAKULYTE SUBTERRA (860 Gs)
BAKU STAND AQUOS (770 Gs)
BAKUSTAND HAOS (800 Gs OR 900 Gs)
BAKUSTAND SUBTERRA (860 Gs)
BAKUSTAND VENTUS (880 Gs)
BLUE-GOLD STEALTH DARKUS (860 Gs)

COREDEM

Did you ever land on a Gate card, ready to battle, and then find out that the card gives your opponent extra power? Gate cards are no problem for this massive monster. He can punch the ground with his huge fists, destroying the Gate card and its powers. Coredem's fists get extra strength from the blue lens on his chest. The lens emits a ray of light that powers up his fists to deliver devastating energy punches.

SEEN WITH: BATTLE BRAWLER JAKE.

AVAILABLE ATTRIBUTES

VENTUS (640 Gs, 650 Gs, OR 770 Gs)

OTHER FORMS

CLEAR (720 Gs)
DEKA VENTUS (680 Gs)
SHADOW DARKUS (760 Gs)

DHARAK

Dharak and Drago share the same DNA, which explains how this Bakugan gets his strength. Their lineage is the most powerful biological makeup of the ancient Bakugans. In battle, Dharak can destroy opponents with a dark energy burst from his mouth.

SEEN WITH: BARODIOUS, EMPEROR OF THE TWELVE ORDERS. DHARAK IS GUNDALDIA'S BAKUGAN, BUT ONLY EMPEROR BARODIUS CAN BRING OUT THE BEST IN HIS ABILITIES.

AVAILABLE ATTRIBUTES

AQUOS (720 Gs OR 780 Gs)

DARKUS (600 Gs, 610 Gs, 700 Gs, 720 Gs, 730 Gs, 750 Gs, OR 790 Gs)

HAOS (640 Gs)

PYRUS (660 Gs)

SUBTERRA (610 Gs, 620 Gs, OR 720 Gs)

VENTUS (700 Gs OR 750 Gs)

OTHER FORMS

DEKA AQUOS (720 Gs)
BLUE-GOLD STEALTH PYRUS (870 Gs)
STONE HAOS (750 Gs)

HAKAPOID

This Bakugan is most at home in the deepest depths of the sea. Hakapoid's huge eye can spot even the smallest prey miles away. If it decides to attack, it will use its super sharp teeth, which can tear through the toughest armor. Hakapoid has hundreds of teeth to do the job. If an enemy attacks, it will have to get past Hakapoid's spikes before it can do any damage.

AVAILABLE ATTRIBUTES

- DARKUS (650 Gs or 780 Gs)
- PYRUS (620 Gs)
- VENTUS (820 Gs)

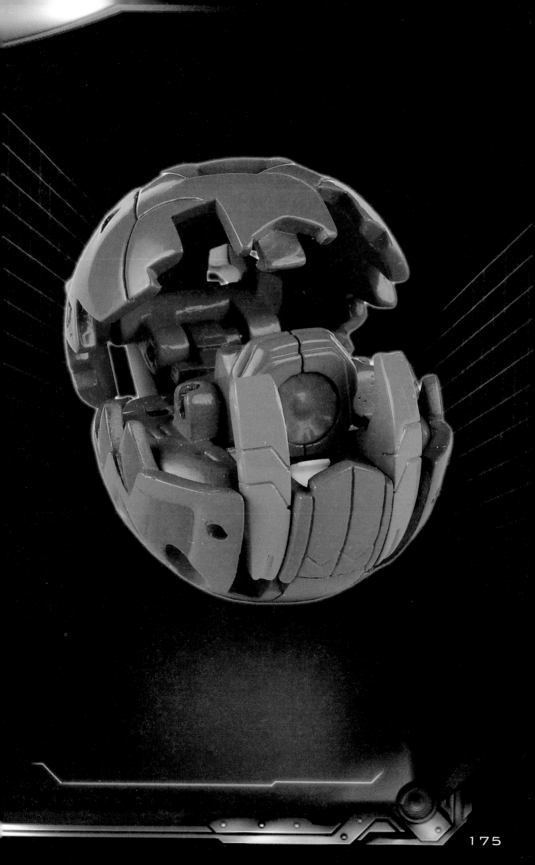

HAWKTOR

This bird-like Bakugan has the flying powers and excellent eyesight of a hawk. In aerial combat, Hawktor swoops, dips, and soars with expert agility. Whether on or off the field, Hawktor takes pride in its abilities. It also has a strong sense of justice, and can always be counted on to do the right thing.

SEEN WITH: BATTLE BRAWLER SHUN.

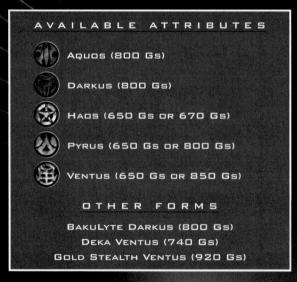

AVAILABLE ATTRIBUTES

AQUOS (800 Gs)

DARKUS (800 Gs)

HAOS (650 Gs or 670 Gs)

PYRUS (650 Gs or 800 Gs)

VENTUS (650 Gs or 850 Gs)

OTHER FORMS

BAKULYTE DARKUS (800 Gs)
DEKA VENTUS (740 Gs)
GOLD STEALTH VENTUS (920 Gs)

HELIX DRAGONOID

Helix Dragonoid gets its awesome power from the DNA of the ancient Bakugans. Like many Dragonoids, Helix Dragonoid can unleash a fiery flame from its mouth that few foes can withstand. And Helix Dragonoid has an extra skill: its mastery of logic and reason. That makes this Bakugan a master strategist on the battlefield.

SEEN WITH: DAN KUSO.

AVAILABLE ATTRIBUTES

- Aquos (620 Gs, 640 Gs, 660 Gs, or 750 Gs)
- Darkus (630 Gs or 740 Gs)
- Haos (630 Gs, 660 Gs, 710 Gs, 730 Gs, or 760 Gs)
- Pyrus (600 Gs, 650 Gs, 690 Gs, 700 Gs, 720 Gs, 730 Gs, 740 Gs, 750Gs, 760 Gs, 800 Gs, or 850 Gs)
- Subterra (740 Gs)
- Ventus (640 Gs, 720 Gs, 750 Gs, and 850 Gs)

OTHER FORMS

Clear (750 Gs, 770 Gs, 850 Gs, 880 Gs, or 900 Gs)
Gold Stealth Haos (900 Gs)
Camouflage Ventus (740 Gs)

FOR EVOLUTION CHAIN, FLIP TO PAGE 17.

KRAKIX

Krakix is one big, beefy warrior. He's brutal on the battlefield, and when he attacks, he shows no mercy to his foes. He's equipped with a suit of armor and a giant ninja star that he carries on his back.

Krakix's attacks are all about fire and heat. He has the ability to create flare swords from both his hands. He can also unleash a giant flame from his mouth to increase both his defense and attack skills.

SEEN WITH: GILL OF THE TWELVE ORDERS.

AVAILABLE ATTRIBUTES

- Darkus (650 Gs, 670 Gs, or 750 Gs)
- Haos (750 Gs)
- Pyrus (670 Gs, 780 Gs, or 800 Gs)
- Subterra (650 Gs)
- Ventus (640 Gs)

OTHER FORMS

Clear (780 Gs)

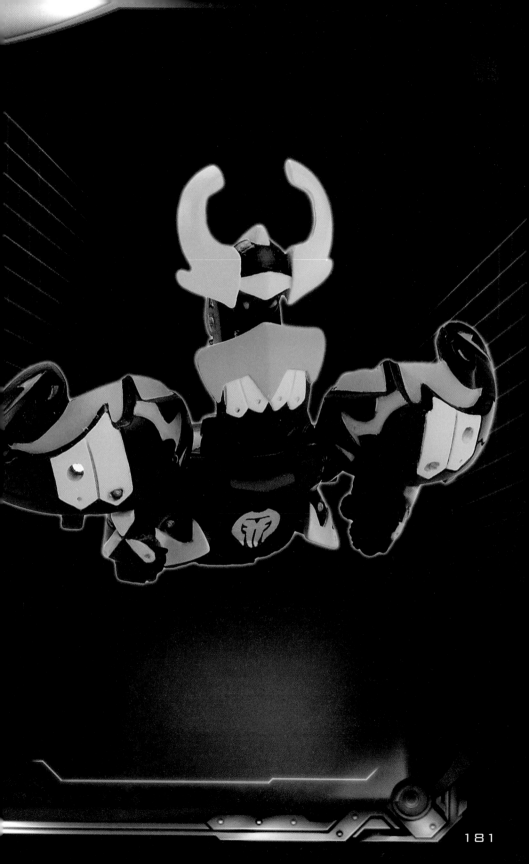

LINEHALT

This mysterious warrior grew up in the dark underground of Gundalia. He has exceptional, almost magical, powers. Linehalt can use a stone in the palm of his hand to absorb and nullify the attacks of his enemies. There are many secrets surrounding this Bakugan. Some say he holds a "forbidden power." Time will tell if this power will be revealed.

SEEN WITH: REN AND HIS TEAM. LINEHALT AND REN SHARE A STRONG BOND THAT INCLUDES BOTH THEIR MEMORIES AND FIERCE DREAMS.

AVAILABLE ATTRIBUTES

DARKUS (750 Gs or 800 Gs)

PYRUS (650 Gs or 850 Gs)

SUBTERRA (640 Gs, 680 Gs, or 800 Gs)

VENTUS (650 Gs or 800 Gs)

OTHER FORMS

BAKULYTE PYRUS (850 Gs)
BAKULYTE VENTUS (800 Gs)
BLUE-GOLD STEALTH SUBTERRA (880 Gs)

LUMAGROWL

This beastly Bakugan's tail is equipped with sharp swords. He can use the swords to attack in all directions from close range. Lumagrowl can also harness the power of lightning. When he spreads his tail in a special way, it will shoot out a strong lightning bolt to paralyze his opponent. Many Bakugan like to trash talk, threaten, or even joke around on the field, but Lumagrowl's not like that. He hardly ever shows emotion, so it's difficult for his partner to know what he's thinking.

SEEN WITH: KAZARINA OF THE TWELVE ORDERS.

AVAILABLE ATTRIBUTES

AQUOS (600 Gs, 700 Gs, 720 Gs, 730 Gs, or 740 Gs)

DARKUS (700 Gs)

HAOS (630 Gs, 660 Gs, or 770 Gs)

PYRUS (650 Gs)

VENTUS (730 Gs or 780 Gs)

OTHER FORMS

CLEAR (700 Gs or 780 Gs)
DEKA GOLD (740 Gs)
ARCTIC CAMOUFLAGE HAOS (790 Gs)

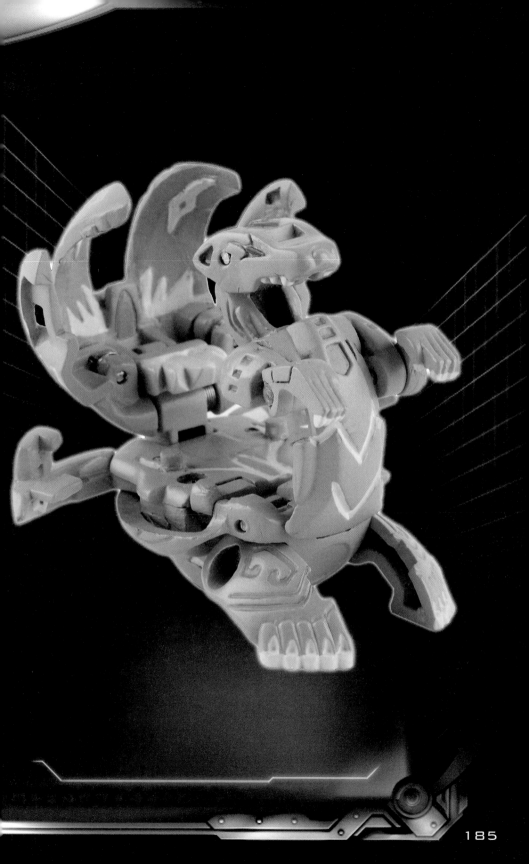

LUMINO DRAGONOID

Better put on your sunglasses! Lumino Dragonoid is one shiny Bakugan. He has four gleaming wings, a tail with twin blades, and a super strong v-neck armored plate to protect his chest.

Like other Dragonoid, Lumino Dragonoid can shoot fireballs from his mouth. But Lumino can power his fireballs with a devastating double charge!

SEEN WITH: DAN KUSO. LUMINO DRAGONOID IS ONE OF THE EVOLVED FORMS OF HIS GUARDIAN BAKUGAN, DRAGO.

AVAILABLE ATTRIBUTES

AQUOS (850 GS OR 880 GS)

DARKUS (700 GS OR 750 GS)

HAOS (750 GS)

PYRUS (750 GS, 810 GS, 870 GS, OR 900 GS)

SUBTERRA (850 GS)

VENTUS (900 GS)

OTHER FORMS

BAKUDOUBLESTRIKE AQUOS (770 GS – DS POWER 30, 770 GS – DS POWER 80, 850 GS – DS POWER 50)

BAKUDOUBLESTRIKE HAOS (750 GS – DS POWER 50)

BAKUDOUBLESTRIKE PYRUS (870 GS – DS POWER 30, 870 GS – DS POWER 80)

BAKUDOUBLESTRIKE VENTUS (750 GS – DS POWER 50, 900 GS – DS POWER 10)

BAKUMETALIX AQUOS (610 GS)

BAKUMETALIX PYRUS (630 GS OR 810 GS)

BAKUMETALIX SUBTERRA (750 GS)

DEKA SILVER (750 GS), DEKA SUBTERRA (740 GS)

LAVA ROCK PYRUS (780 GS)

FOR EVOLUTION CHAIN, FLIP TO PAGE 17.

LYTHIRUS

This Bakugan combines the attack styles of insects, reptiles, and fish. He's normally calm, but it doesn't take much to make Lythirus angry. And when that happens, watch out!

An angry Lythirus is ferocious and savage and will go on a destructive rampage. He'll cut up anything in his path with his scissor-like hands. Lythirus will do anything at all to win—no matter what dirty trick he has to use to get the job done.

SEEN WITH: STOICA OF THE TWELVE ORDERS.

AVAILABLE ATTRIBUTES

AQUOS (650 Gs, 700 Gs, or 850 Gs)

DARKUS (640 Gs or 800 Gs)

HAOS (850 Gs)

PYRUS (800 Gs)

SUBTERRA (630 Gs)

VENTUS (800 Gs)

OTHER FORMS

BAKULYTE AQUOS (850 Gs)
BAKULYTE PYRUS (800 Gs)
DEKA AQUOS (760 Gs)
GOLD STEALTH AQUOS (910 Gs)

PHOSPHOS

Ren is a crafty Bakugan with a cheeky sense of humor. But the
nothing funny about his attacks! He can spit toxic venom fron
mouth to decrease his opponent's energy levels. But that's not al
Phosphos has long, stretchable nails he can use to rip his foes to

SEEN WITH: REN. PHOSPHOS IS PART OF REN'S TEAM

AVAILABLE ATTRIBUTES

Aquos (740 Gs or 750 Gs)

Pyrus (770 Gs)

OTHER FORMS

BakuDoublestrike Haos (680 Gs – DS Power 70,
860 Gs – DS Power 40)
BakuDoublestrike Pyrus (790 Gs – DS Power 60)
BakuDoublestrike Ventus (670 Gs – DS Power 30,
670 Gs – DS Power 80)
BakuMetalix Darkus (650 Gs)
BakuMetalix Pyrus (760 Gs)
BakuMetalix Ventus (750 Gs)

PLITHEON

This outlaw Bakugan lives to fight. His battle style is a combination of cool strategy and vicious attacks. Plitheon will use any method necessary to win a battle. He's strong and aggressive on the field, and he uses unusual battle plans to maintain that energy—and take down every opponent in his path.

SEEN WITH: REN. PLITHEON IS PART OF REN'S TEAM.

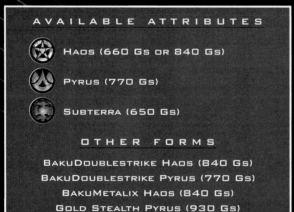

AVAILABLE ATTRIBUTES

Haos (660 Gs or 840 Gs)

Pyrus (770 Gs)

Subterra (650 Gs)

OTHER FORMS

BakuDoublestrike Haos (840 Gs)
BakuDoublestrike Pyrus (770 Gs)
BakuMetalix Haos (840 Gs)
Gold Stealth Pyrus (930 Gs)

RUBANOID

Rubanoid is a striking figure on the field in his crimson armor. It may look cool, but it also protects him from attacks. This Bakugan's opponents hope his armor is the only red they'll see—when Rubanoid attacks, he shoots red energy waves from his mouth! Rubanoid can also pound foes with his sharp claws.

SEEN WITH: REN. RUBANOID IS PART OF REN'S TEAM.

AVAILABLE ATTRIBUTES

AQUOS (620 Gs OR 770 Gs)

DARKUS (650 Gs, 750 Gs, OR 850 Gs)

HAOS (630 Gs OR 790 Gs)

PYRUS (750 Gs)

SUBTERRA (800 Gs)

VENTUS (630 Gs)

OTHER FORMS

BAKUEXOSKIN DARKUS (750 Gs, 850 Gs, 790 Gs, OR 920 Gs)
BAKUEXOSKIN HAOS (790 Gs, 800 Gs, OR 900 Gs)
BAKUEXOSKIN SUBTERRA (800 Gs)
BLUE-GOLD STEALTH VENTUS (890 Gs)

SABATOR

Sabator has a wild personality and likes to take risks, but his attacks are grounded in the earth at his feet. He can manipulate the energy of the ground to unleash attacks from every direction. Sabator uses power more than strategy on the field. One of his favorite moves is to get the drills on his shoulders spinning and then charge his opponent.

SEEN WITH: NURZAK OF THE TWELVE ORDERS.

AVAILABLE ATTRIBUTES

- Aquos (630 Gs)
- Haos (650 Gs)
- Subterra (670 Gs, 740 Gs, 750 Gs, 760 Gs, 800 Gs, 820 Gs, or 830 Gs)
- Ventus (760 Gs, 770 Gs, or 800 Gs)

OTHER FORMS

Clear (760 Gs)

Desert Camouflage (800 Gs)

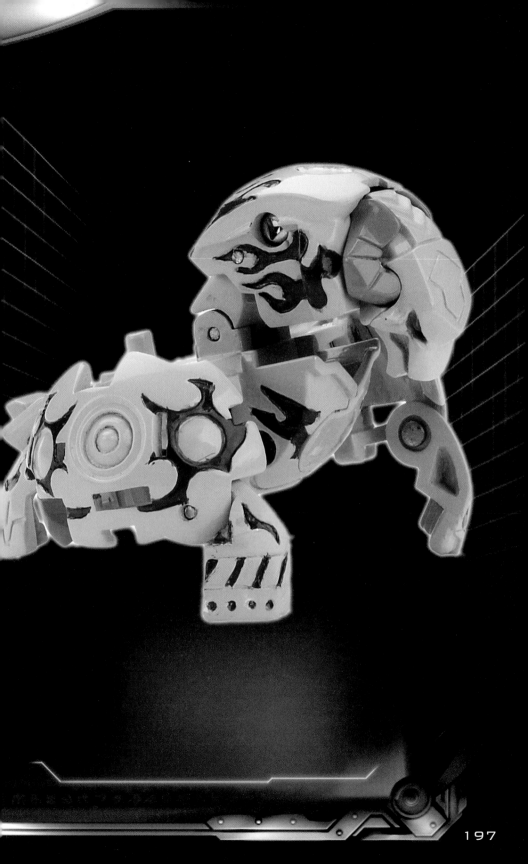

SNAPZOID

Whatever you do, stay away from Snapzoid's mouth! Not only does this vicious Bakugan have a venomous bite, he has an extra mouth that will emerge to attack! If Snapzoid doesn't bite you, he'll zap you with the electrically charged whips on his body.

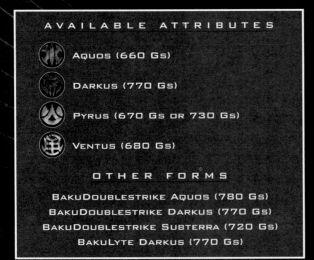

AVAILABLE ATTRIBUTES

AQUOS (660 Gs)

DARKUS (770 Gs)

PYRUS (670 Gs OR 730 Gs)

VENTUS (680 Gs)

OTHER FORMS

BAKUDOUBLESTRIKE AQUOS (780 Gs)
BAKUDOUBLESTRIKE DARKUS (770 Gs)
BAKUDOUBLESTRIKE SUBTERRA (720 Gs)
BAKULYTE DARKUS (770 Gs)

STRIKEFLIER

This master battler is full of tricks. He can transform himself freely on the field. Strikeflier can also absorb his opponent's abilities, and then combine them to strengthen his own abilities. You could say he's a real ability thief!

SEEN WITH: AIRZEL OF THE TWELVE ORDERS.

AVAILABLE ATTRIBUTES

- AQUOS (650 Gs, 680 Gs, 690 Gs, or 800 Gs)
- DARKUS (630 Gs or 730 Gs)
- HAOS (630 Gs, 740 Gs, or 770 Gs)
- PYRUS (750 Gs)
- SUBTERRA (600 Gs or 630 Gs)
- VENTUS (660 Gs, 750 Gs, or 780 Gs)

OTHER FORMS
CLEAR (780 Gs)
STONE HAOS (770 Gs)

BAKUGAN BATTLE GEAR

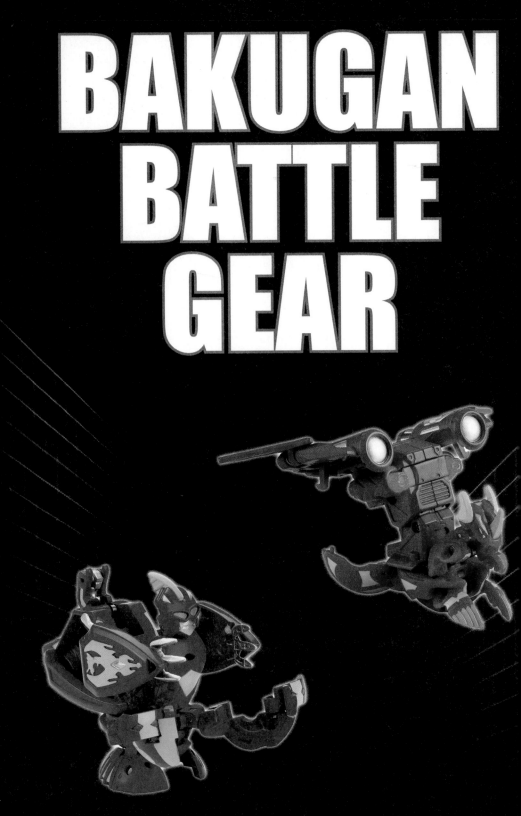

With Bakugan Battle Gear, you can defeat your opponents like never before! Battle Gear aren't Bakugan—they're extreme accessories that attach to your Bakugan, giving them an extra power boost.

If defense is what you need, there is Battle Gear that acts as protective armor. And if you want to increase your offensive power, there's plenty of Battle Gear for that. You can choose from an impressive array of battle cannons, sharp blades, blasters, lasers, and even jet engines.

So if you're looking to raise through the ranks of Bakugan Brawlers, some Battle Gear might be just what you need. Your opponents won't know what hit them!

OR

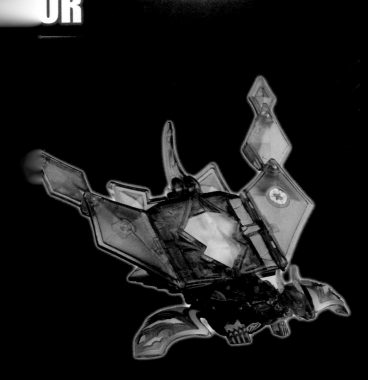

This gear allows any Bakugan to take flight. The metal wings attach to a Bakugan monster, allowing it to fly at super speed. The wings can rotate so the Bakugan can hover in midair. They're also super strong, so they can withstand multiple blows without breaking. When you equip your Bakugan with Airkor, you get an added bonus. This gear discharges giant energy bolts to electrify your foes!

AVAILABLE ELEMENT COLORS

Copper (60 Gs or 70 Gs)

Gold (50 Gs or 70 Gs)

Silver (70 Gs or 120 Gs)

BARIAS GEAR

These disks are made of a combination of two strong, light metals melded together. Because the disks are lightweight, your Bakugan can aim them at opponents with expert accuracy and speed. But they're also strong enough to be used as body armor.

Barias Gear also includes a flash laser cannon. One blast from this can nullify all of your opponent's abilities!

AVAILABLE ELEMENT COLORS

Copper (70 Gs)

Gold (80 Gs)

BATTLE CRUSHER

When an item has "crusher" in its name, you know it can deliver maximum damage! Battle Crusher is a mega-cannon blaster that fires powerful energy beams. There's an auto lock target feature, so the blaster can fire multiple shots in a row. But the Battle Crusher is about more than just brute power—it's smart. It contains a directional defense system to protect itself from attacks. It can also upgrade itself automatically on command.

AVAILABLE ELEMENT COLORS

Copper (80 Gs or 100 Gs)

Gold (90 Gs)

Silver (80 Gs)

BATTLE SABRE

The secret to this gear is the specially tempered steel that makes up the two sharp blades of the sabre. It won't rust underwater. It's lightweight, so it's easy to use and control. And if you're engaged in a long battle, the blades don't need to be resharpened.

AVAILABLE ELEMENT COLORS

COPPER (100 Gs)

GOLD (90 Gs)

SILVER (80 Gs)

LE TURBINE

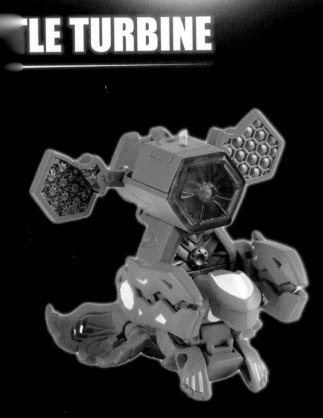

The Battle Turbine is a teriffic defensive weapon. Those big blasters on its side shoot out anti-missile defense beams to keep your Bakugan safe from attack. It comes equipped with turbines that generate constant power so you'll never lose steam during a battle.

AVAILABLE ELEMENT COLORS

Copper (70 Gs or 130 Gs)

Gold (70 Gs)

Silver (60 Gs or 80 Gs)

BOOMIX

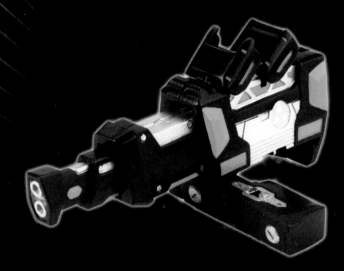

It takes a super strong Bakugan to wield Boomix. It's the longest and heaviest of all the battle cannons. But if you've got the muscle, then Boomix can't be beat as an offensive weapon. It fires guided lasers that can target an enemy under the most difficult conditions. Even if your foe is far away, Boomix's beams will lock on and hit their mark.

AVAILABLE ELEMENT COLORS

COPPER (80 Gs OR 210 Gs)

GOLD (50 Gs, 80 Gs, OR 200 Gs)

SILVER (50 Gs, 70 Gs, OR 200 Gs)

CHOMPIXX

Just the sight of these two giant, deadly blades is enough to send an opponent running for cover. When these blades chomp into the ground, they unleash their incredible energy. The ground breaks open, swallowing anything in its path. Chompixx also comes equipped with is own double-sided axe.

AVAILABLE ELEMENT COLORS

Copper (60 Gs, 70 Gs, or 90 Gs)

Gold (50 Gs or 80 Gs)

Silver (70 Gs or 100 Gs)

JE

What's better than one battle cannon? How about two! Jetkor's twin cannons can take down an enemy with a double blast. This gear has a lock-on beam that shoots from a green lens to freeze an opponent before the blast hits, making it easier to target. It also comes with a giant jet pack with enough fuel to circle the Earth more than once without refueling.

AVAILABLE ELEMENT COLORS

Copper (60 Gs or 70 Gs)

Gold (70 Gs)

Silver (50 Gs, 70 Gs, or 80 Gs)

OTHER FORMS

Deka Silver (50 Gs)

)R

or fans of close combat, Lansor is a key piece of gear. This long spear can be thrown for long distances or used to thrust into a foe's armor at close range. The long pole extends for greater range, and the unbreakable tip can penetrate the toughest materials. There's even a shield at the base that can be used for defense.

AVAILABLE ELEMENT COLORS

Copper (90 Gs)

Gold (100 Gs)

ROCK HAM

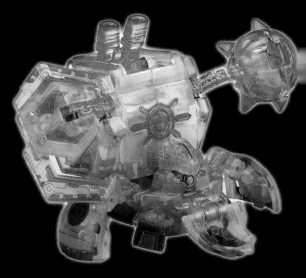

s your opponent's Gate card giving him an extra power boost? Then use Rock Hammer's double blasters—they'll wipe out the effects of the card in one blow. But that's not all Rockhammer can do. It can combine a large axe and iron ball to become a huge energy cannon. It also has a massive claw that can lift opponents on the field and toss them aside.

AVAILABLE ELEMENT COLORS

COPPER (70 Gs)

GOLD (70 Gs OR 120 Gs)

SILVER (60 Gs)

OTHER FORMS

DEKA COPPER (50 Gs)

ORCREST

Tired of getting blasted by laser beams? Terrorcrest's armor will protect your Bakugan. It can intercept lasers or rockets in mid-air, or deflect a blow from a foe's fierce fist. Terrorcrest's shield can also be used for offense. The poison-filled claws can grow longer and sharper during battle, delivering deadly damage with one swipe.

AVAILABLE ELEMENT COLORS

Copper (90 Gs or 100 Gs)

Gold (90 Gs)

Silver (60 Gs, 100 Gs, or 110 Gs)

TWIN DESTRU[C]

First, Twin Destructor tracks opponents as they race, dodge, or fly across the battlefield. Then, it fires with its Vulcan laser, pounding opponents with a double dose of damage.

AVAILABLE ELEMENT COLORS

Copper (100 Gs)

Gold (90 Gs)

Silver (100 Gs)

...ITOR GEAR

Does your big Bakugan need a boost? This gear has two large jet engines powerful enough to lift heavy Bakugan off of the ground. Then they can swoop down from high altitudes for high attacks. Vilantor Gear also comes with multiple fire blasting barrels that shoot out energy attacks. The attacks have the combined power of tornado winds and lightning strikes.

AVAILABLE ELEMENT COLORS

Copper (90 Gs or 130 Gs)

Gold (80 Gs or 120 Gs)

Silver (80 Gs, 90 Gs, or 120 Gs)

ZUKAN

Want to add some fire to your attacks? Then strap this on to the back of your Bakugan and get ready to launch blasts of red-hot magma! Zukanator uses four red laser beam pointers to increase accuracy. It has a silencer on the tip to reduce noise, making this gear perfect for surprise attacks.

AVAILABLE ELEMENT COLORS

Copper (80 Gs or 210 Gs)

Gold (60 Gs, 90 Gs, or 200 Gs)

Silver (70 Gs or 200 Gs)

What do you do when you need to boost your battle brawling arsenal? Add some Bakugan Super Assault and surprise your opponents with their extra abilities. Each Bakugan Super Assault has a unique design and comes with one metal Gate card and one Ability card.

The Bakuzoom feature empowers a Bakugan with extra speed and ability. Looking to confuse and confound your opponents? Then a Bakuchance Bakugan might be for you. With Bakubolt, a Bakugan Super Assault can blind an enemy with glowing light. Bakugan with Bakuvice can crush opponents in a powerful grip. And the Bakutremor and Bakucyclone features harness the power of nature to create earthquake-like vibrations and destructive winds on the battlefield.

No two Bakugan Super Assault are alike. How do you know which is best for you? Get one on your team and test them out in battle!

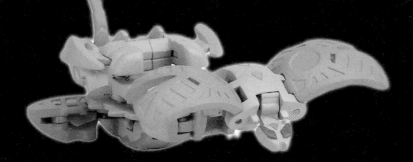

APEXEON

When Apexeon strikes, look out! Its fierce fangs deliver a venomous bite. Apexeon has metal spider-like legs that enable it to maneuver quickly around the field. The blades on the end of its feet can cut through armor.

SPECIAL ATTACK FEATURE

BAKUBOLT

AQUOS (800 Gs)

DARKUS (810 Gs)

BREEZAK

This mighty Bakugan is known for its strong moves on the field. Opponents fear its three sharp claws, which can slash through the toughest body armor. If Breezak is attacked from behind, foes have to avoid a barrier of sharp spikes.

SPECIAL ATTACK FEATURE

BakuZoom

Aquos (810 Gs)

Darkus (780 Gs)

Haos (910 Gs)

Pyrus (800 Gs)

Ventus (790 Gs)

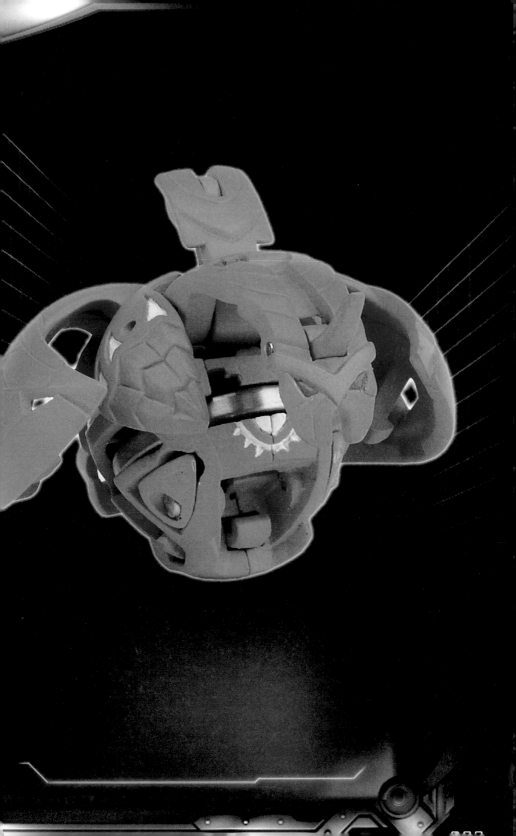

CHANCE DRAGONOID

Chance Dragonoid is all about might and power on the field. Its body is massive, with sharp thorns on its back to protect it from sneak attacks. It needs four huge wings to lift its body into the sky. Those wings are so strong that when they flap, they create a forceful gust of wind. This Bakugan also has four powerful claws that make it easy to battle two foes at once.

SPECIAL ATTACK FEATURE

BakuChance
(Roll to determine one of several possible G-Powers)

Aquos: 850 – 750 – 650 – 600 – 550 – or 350 Gs

Darkus: 860 – 700 –500 – or 400 Gs

Haos: 820 – 770 – 700 – 600 – 500 – or 400 Gs

Pyrus: 900 – 750 – 700 – 600 – 500 – or 400 Gs

Pyrus: 850 – 700 – 650 – 550 – 500 – or 400 Gs

Subterra: 800 – 780 – 750 – 700 – 500 – 300 Gs

Ventus: 820 – 730 – 670 – 600 – 530 – or 450 Gs

Ventus: 870 – 750 – 700 – 600 – 500 – or 450 Gs

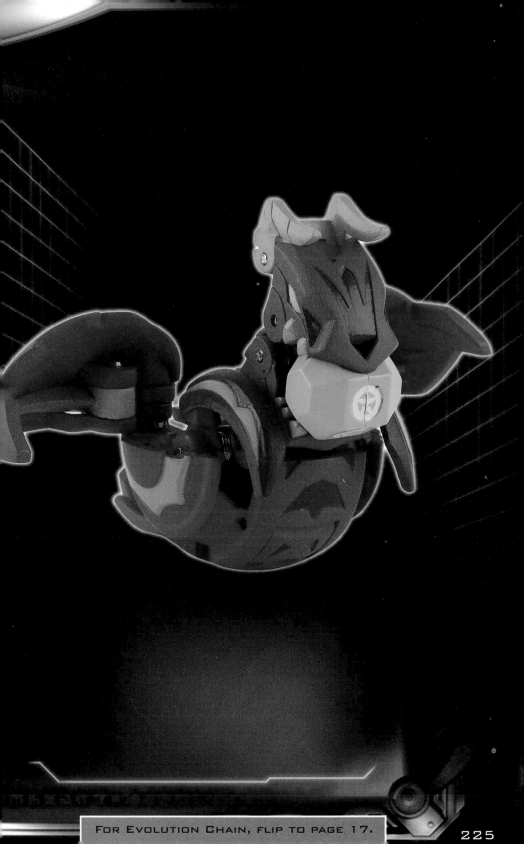

FOR EVOLUTION CHAIN, FLIP TO PAGE 17.

CLAWSAURUS

This Bakugan can use just about every part of its body during a battle. It can stick out its long tongue and grab opponents with the pincers on its tip. It lashes out at foes with its long tail. When it's fighting tall Bakugan, it can stand firmly on its back legs to face them. Finally, its strongest feature is its big tusk, which can grip an enemy tightly and then toss it aside. This Bakugan has one weakness—it's normally low to the ground and it can't fly, so flying Bakugan can attack it from above. But once the enemy gets close enough to Clawsaurus's powerful tail, the advantage is gone.

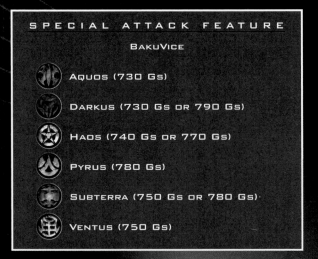

SPECIAL ATTACK FEATURE

BAKUVICE

AQUOS (730 Gs)

DARKUS (730 Gs or 790 Gs)

HAOS (740 Gs or 770 Gs)

PYRUS (780 Gs)

SUBTERRA (750 Gs or 780 Gs)·

VENTUS (750 Gs)

COBRAKUS

This Bakugan has a heavy metal body that can withstand the toughest punishment. Cobrakus has a rotating barrel in the center of its snake-like body to shoot at its opponents. When it gets an enemy in its grasp, it will fiercely shake it until it weakens. Then Cobrakus strikes—with one final, poisonous bite!

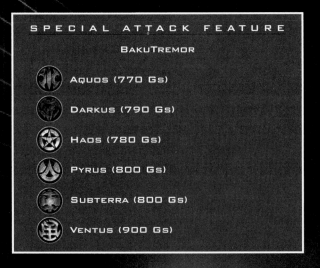

SPECIAL ATTACK FEATURE

BakuTremor

- Aquos (770 Gs)
- Darkus (790 Gs)
- Haos (780 Gs)
- Pyrus (800 Gs)
- Subterra (800 Gs)
- Ventus (900 Gs)

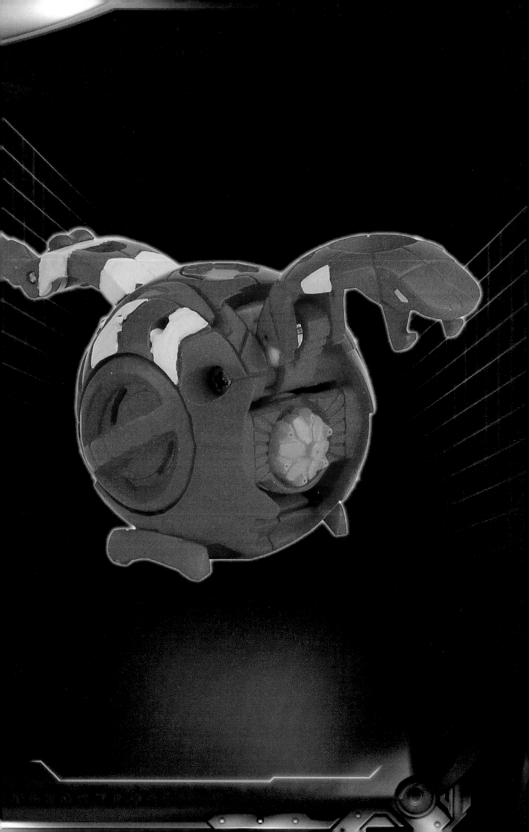

FARAKSPIN

Farakspin gets most of its power from its four fast-spinning wings. They enable it to fly long distances without having to stop and rest. And when they rotate fast enough, they can create a whirling tornado! This Bakugan is small, so it's difficult to catch. Farakspin has one other advantage: it can see in the dark, thanks to its red eyes. That means it can battle day or night.

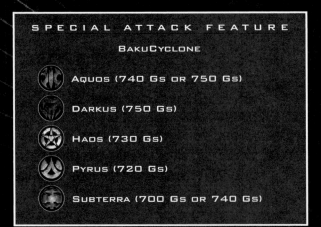

SPECIAL ATTACK FEATURE

BAKUCYCLONE

AQUOS (740 Gs OR 750 Gs)

DARKUS (750 Gs)

HAOS (730 Gs)

PYRUS (720 Gs)

SUBTERRA (700 Gs OR 740 Gs)

GLOTRONOID

Some Bakugan rely on brute force to beat down foes. Not Glotronoid. Its powers are more mysterious. Glotronoid would rather confuse its enemies than pound them. First, it can produce an intense glow from its body to blind rivals during combat. Next, it sprays a poisonous venom that makes anyone who breathes it disoriented. And if that's not enough, Glotronoid emits a silent, ultrasonic wave that controls the minds of its opponents, forcing them to fight against each other!

SPECIAL ATTACK FEATURE

BakuBolt

Subterra (750 Gs)

Ventus (760 Gs)

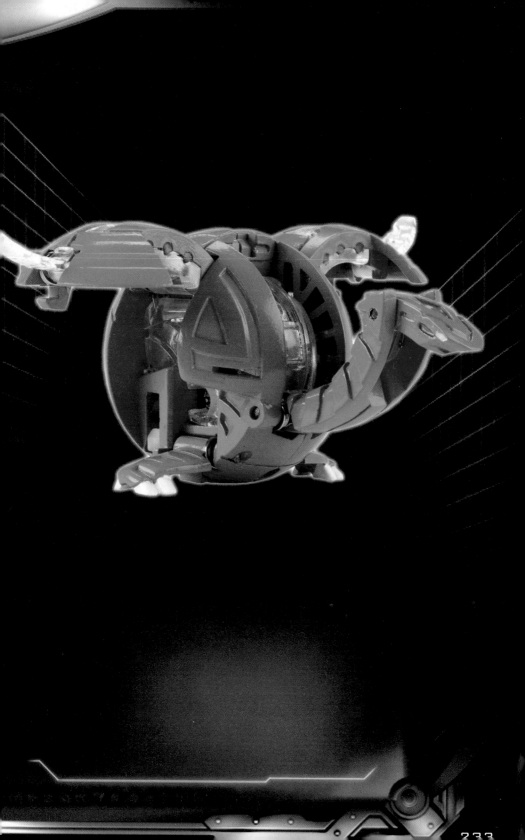

LONGFLY

This Bakugan relies on the powers of its six mighty wings to dominate in battle. The wings allow Longfly to soar at super speed, and his stealthy shape allows him to attack before a rival Bakugan knows what hit him. If Longfly shakes his wings while hovering over the ground, he unleashes a massive shockwave to send opponents sprawling!

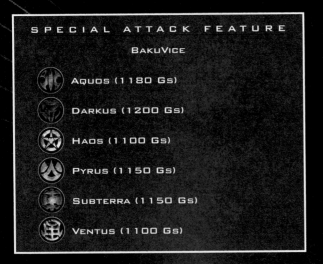

SPECIAL ATTACK FEATURE

BAKUVICE

AQUOS (1180 GS)

DARKUS (1200 GS)

HAOS (1100 GS)

PYRUS (1150 GS)

SUBTERRA (1150 GS)

VENTUS (1100 GS)

LUMITROID

This Super Assault Bakugan resembles an insect. Just about every part of its body is built for attack. Its long tail can wrap around opponents at close range or shoot a spear from a distance with spot-on aim. Its four legs allow Lumitroid to maneuver expertly around the battlefield. And its eyes can shine so brightly that the glow will stop a foe in its tracks.

SPECIAL ATTACK FEATURE

BAKUBOLT

PYRUS (730 Gs)

HAOS (750 Gs)

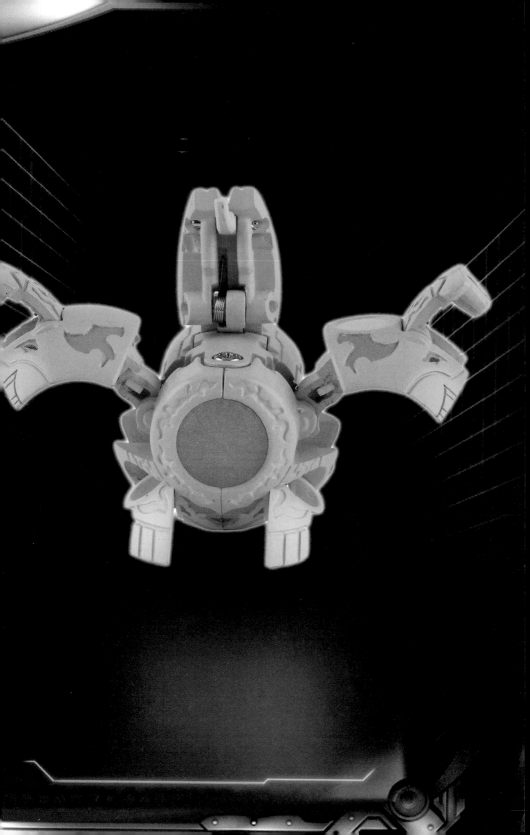

MERLIX

Merlix resembles a magician or wizard with massive muscles. But Merlix rarely relies on brute force to win a battle. Instead, he uses the power of his mind. His Bakugan can read the minds of his foes and then confuse them by creating a vision that's the opposite of what they're thinking. That will cause the opponent to make a bad move. The cloak Merlix wears adds to his mysterious aura, but it's useful, too. It can protect him from most kinds of damage.

SPECIAL ATTACK FEATURE

BakuChance
(Roll to determine one of several possible G-Powers)

Aquos: 950 – 800 – 750 – 650 – 500 – or 400 Gs

Darkus: 750 – 700 – 700 – 650 – 600 – or 500 Gs

Pyrus: 990 – 880 – 770 – 660 – 550 – or 440 Gs

Pyrus: 750 – 700 – 650 – 600 – or 500 Gs

Pyrus: 750 – 700 – 680 – 600 – 580 – or 550 Gs

MYSTIC CHANCER

Mystic Chancer is equipped to withstand damage. He can use his quarterstaff to block enemy attacks. The metal shields he wears protect his chest and legs from harm. When Mystic Chancer attacks, he uses his three-pronged tail. With it, he can battle two attackers at a time.

SPECIAL ATTACK FEATURE

BakuChance
(ROLL TO DETERMINE ONE OF SEVERAL POSSIBLE G-POWERS)

Darkus: 940 – 810 – 800 – 650 – 500 – or 100 Gs

Haos: 750 – 650 – 500 – 350 – or 300 Gs

Pyrus: 800 – 650 – 500 – 450 – or 400 Gs

Subterra: 960 – 770 – 700 – 700 – 600 – or 500 Gs

Ventus: 850 – 750 – 500 – 450 – 400 – or 300 Gs

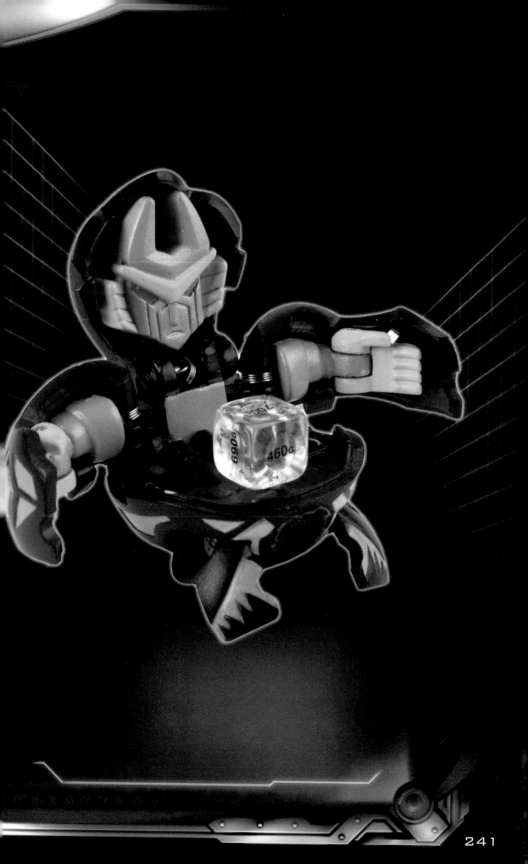

QUAKE DRAGONOID

This Super Assault Bakugan rages with intensity on the battlefield! He stomps around slowly and steadily, and then—bam! He attacks with a powerful punch. If Quake Dragonoid punches the ground, the shockwaves are so strong they can start an avalanche. If Quake Dragonoid needs to boost his attack, he can shoot a fire blast from his mouth. The heat is so intense it can melt and destroy anything in his path!

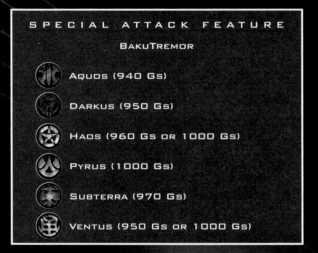

SPECIAL ATTACK FEATURE

BAKUTREMOR

AQUOS (940 Gs)

DARKUS (950 Gs)

HAOS (960 Gs OR 1000 Gs)

PYRUS (1000 Gs)

SUBTERRA (970 Gs)

VENTUS (950 Gs OR 1000 Gs)

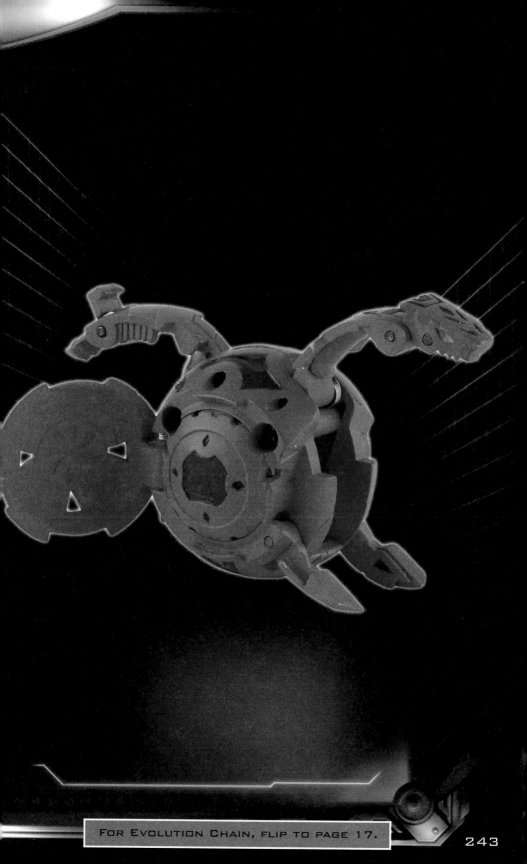

FOR EVOLUTION CHAIN, FLIP TO PAGE 17.

RAPTORIX

Like a chameleon, Raptorix can blend into his surroundings. When prey is near, he can launch a surprise attack. This Bakugan can also use his cloaking ability to project intense green images onto the sky. This confuses his rivals, giving Raptorix the advantage he needs to gain victory. Raptorix may be lizard-like, but he's no friendly pet. In fact, he's known for his violent temper. When angry, he'll try to rip apart a foe with his bare hands!

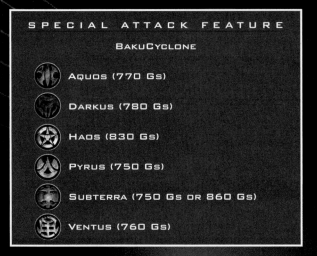

SPECIAL ATTACK FEATURE

BAKUCYCLONE

AQUOS (770 Gs)

DARKUS (780 Gs)

HAOS (830 Gs)

PYRUS (750 Gs)

SUBTERRA (750 Gs OR 860 Gs)

VENTUS (760 Gs)

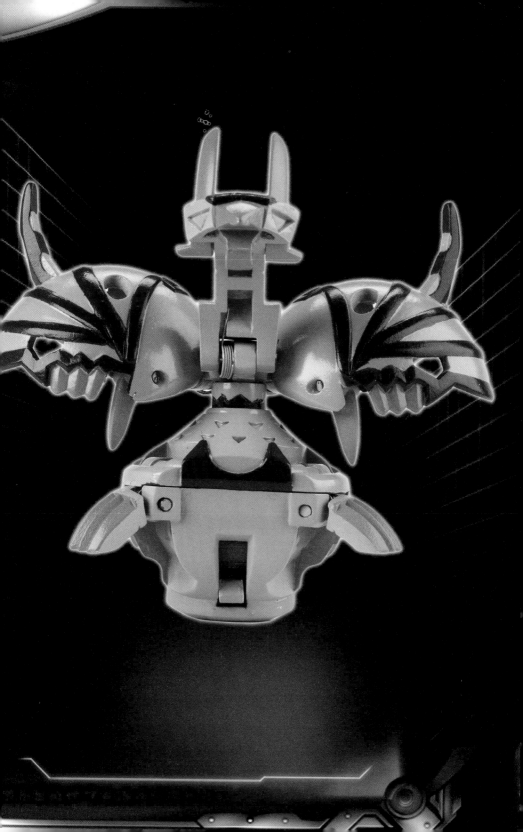

SPLIGHT

Splight's opponents don't know where he will appear next. That's because he has the ability to turn invisible. Then he'll suddenly appear and slash at foes with his sharp claws. If his opponent tries to attack his claws, the blow will be blocked by the strong shields Splight has on the back of each hand. Splight also has guards on his shoulders. He uses those to drive challengers to their knees. If a foe strikes back quickly, Splight will use his long legs to jump out of the way.

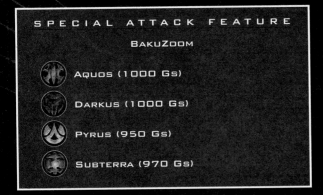

SPECIAL ATTACK FEATURE

BakuZoom

Aquos (1000 Gs)

Darkus (1000 Gs)

Pyrus (950 Gs)

Subterra (970 Gs)

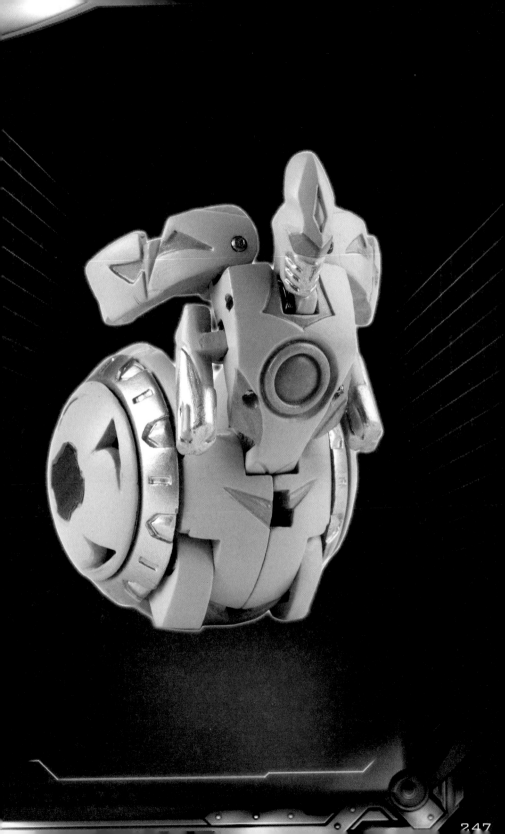

In the battle to save Earth from the Gundalian Invaders, two Bakugan tower above the rest. Dan's Drago is the champion protecting Earth, Emperor Barodius's champion is another Dragonoid, Dharak.

Drago and Dharak share DNA, but they are different at the core. Like the two sides of yin and yang, one fights for the light, while the other has a heart of darkness. When two Bakugan are so opposite yet so evenly matched, it's almost impossible to predict who will win the day.

Now you can recreate their apocalyptic battle with their ultimate forms: Dragonoid Colossus and Dharak Colossus. Each Bakugan is combined with exclusive gear and one exclusive Bakugan to transform into a brand-new, ultra-powerful monster. Turn the page to see everything it takes to put together these Colossus creatures!

DRAGONOID COLOSSUS

t takes five exclusive Bakugan to create Dragonoid Colossus. First, four different kinds of battle gear are added to Dragonoid: Blasteroid, Beamblitzer, Nukix Gear, and Axator Gear. Finally, the Bakugan Battalix Dragonoid is dropped into the Transformation Hub. This triggers an amazing auto-transformation and Dragonoid morphs into his Colossus form.

DHARAK COLOSSUS

Like Dragonoid Colossus, Dharak Colossus is created by combining exclusive battle gear and one exclusive Bakugan. Smashtor, Riptor, and Exokor are added to Dharak's basic form. When Brawlacus Dharak drops into the Transformation Hub, Dharak Colossus comes to life.